MW00532009

Conquering her Heart

(#8 A Forbidden Love Novella Series)

Also By Bree

Historical Romance:

Suspenseful Contemporary Romance:

Middle Grade Adventure:

Paranormal Fantasy:

Conquering her Heart

(#8 A Forbidden Love Novella Series)

by
Bree Wolf

Conquering her Heart

A Regency Romance

By

Bree Wolf

This is a work of fiction. Names, characters, businesses, places, brands, media, events and incidents are either the products of the author's imagination or used in a fictitious manner.

Any resemblance to actual persons, living or dead, or actual events is purely coincidental.

Cover Art by Victoria Cooper

Copyright © 2018 Sabrina Wolf

www.breewolf.com

ISBN-13: 978-3-96482-036-5

All Rights Reserved

This book or any portion thereof may not be reproduced or used in any manner whatsoever without the express written permission of the author except for the use of brief quotations in a book review.

To Monique Takens

A wonderful beta reader with lots of smarts and eyes like a hawk

ACKNOWLEDGEMENTS

A great big thank-you to all those who inspire me daily, those who tell me to keep writing, those who laugh and cry with my characters and me. I love being a writer, and I could never sit down every day to do what I love without all of you. Thank you.

Conquering her Heart

PROLOGUE

On the road to London, spring 1820 (or a variation thereof)

T he world looked different through a curtain of tears.

Gritting her jaw, Abigail Abbott—recently orphaned at the ripe age of nineteen—kept her gaze fixed out the window of the moving carriage, blinking her eyes fiercely to dispel the tears that seemed to fall of their own accord at any time of the day.

Would they ever stop?

Silence hung in the air—uncomfortable silence—and Abigail risked a glance at her aunt Mara, the Dowager Marchioness of Bradish, who sat with her head bowed, her hands linked in her lap, on the other side of the carriage. Not a single word had left her lips since they had set off, and Abigail wondered at the timid-looking woman she had never met before.

Instantly, Abigail's thoughts drifted to the man who had sent Mara—his son's widow—to fetch her to London: Abigail's grandfather, the Duke of Ashold.

Only when asked—begged!—had Abigail's father spoken of the man who had refused his consent, forcing his only daughter to steal away in the night to marry the man she loved. Cold and distant, he had not cared about his daughter's love, her happiness, her wishes. No, among the ton, marriages were forged, based on different aspects, and Abigail's father had been a mere solicitor with hardly a penny to his name.

To this day—even now that he was dead—Abigail could hear the regret and pain over what had happened before her birth in her father's voice, for it had been swiftly followed by an even greater tragedy. Only days after giving birth to their beloved daughter, her mother succumbed to childbed fever. Not even then had her father received word—any word!—from the man who had forced them into hiding. Had he not cared? If so, then why would he send for her—his granddaughter!—now?

Only a week after her father's passing, Abigail had found herself sitting in the small parlour of their home, her gaze drifting over her father's books, neatly sorted and lovingly cared for, a representation of the man himself.

Hours had passed as Abigail had stared into nothing, feeling strangely numb and, yet restless. Sitting idly in a chair was not something she had been accustomed to. After falling ill about two years before, her father had slowly grown worse. No remedy had been able to improve his health, let alone cure him, and as a dutiful and devoted daughter, Abigail had waited on him hand and foot, taking care of their household as before while also seeing to her father as well as his few clients. She had helped him draw up documents, delivered messages and prepared the few consultations with paying clients.

Despite the looming sadness, Abigail's life had been busy from sunup to sundown.

Now, that was over.

For a week she had mostly sat in her father's armchair, not lifting a finger, her eyes red-rimmed from the constant flow of tears. Grief and loss had squeezed her heart, and still, she had noticed the small stabs of fear that assaulted her whenever she dared to think of the future.

What was to happen to her now?

With both her parents gone and no family to speak of, Abigail had been near yielding to despair when a soft knock had sounded on her door.

There, on their front stoop, had stood a finely, though

inconspicuously dressed woman, her gaze soft and fleeting, her hands afflicted by a slight tremble. When she had opened her mouth to introduce herself, her voice had come out as a mere whisper.

Abigail's head had started to spin when she had realised what was happening. Bidding her aunt inside, she had listened silently as the dowager marchioness had extended her grandfather's condolences. "His grace was saddened to hear of your father's passing and bade me come here post-haste to extend an invitation to join him in London."

Swallowing, Abigail had accepted her grandfather's invitation. However, she did not doubt that her aunt's words had been far from the ones the duke had uttered. From what she had learnt of his character from her father, Abigail doubted that the man would ever *ask*. No, he was a duke. He would not ask. He would simply order and expect everyone to do as he bid.

Judging from the apprehensive look in her aunt's eyes, Abigail thought that the duke had never seen one of his *requests* refused.

For that reason alone, Abigail had felt tempted to do just that. However, her current situation did not allow her to choose without regard. No, if she did not wish to end up on the streets, she needed to accept her grandfather's *hospitality*. Perhaps, this would be a chance to learn more of the mother she had never met.

Once more glancing across the carriage at her aunt, Abigail heard her father's words echo in her ears: *Use your head wisely, Child, for it is your greatest ally. One who will never abandon you.*

"Aunt Mara," Abigail began, cringing slightly at the croak in her voice, "may I ask you a question?"

Her aunt's gaze rose from the floor of the carriage, her eyes widening as though she had just received a small shock. "Certainly, my dear."

Abigail frowned. Was she not supposed to address her aunt like that? Would it have been more appropriate to call her *my lady*?

After growing up far from any kind of upper society, Abigail could not recall the correct form of address, and quite frankly after what she had been through, it seemed a silly thing to focus on. After all, this was her family—however, strained their relationship might be—and she would address them in the same respectful but personal way she had always addressed her beloved father.

"Do you know why Grandfather suddenly sent for me?" she asked, welcoming the chance to speak to someone after a week of mourning her father's passing in solitude. "I've never even received a letter from him. I admit this is all very strange."

Aunt Mara swallowed, her pale eyes gentle as they looked at Abigail. "I cannot say what his grace's motivations might have been," she said in a quiet voice. "I am certain you will receive your answers once we arrive in London." A slight shiver shook her frame as though the thought of arriving back at her father-in-law's house terrified her beyond imagining.

Abigail frowned. "I assume grandfather is not a kind man, is he?"

Instantly, her aunt's eyes flew open, and her cheeks turned as white as a sheet. "I would never say such a thing, my dear. He is…he is…He likes everything a certain way. He is fond of order and structure and routine. Nothing is left to chance." Swallowing, her aunt seemed to be groping for words. "To some, his ways might appear cold-h…hearted, but I can assure you he is a most respectful gentleman."

Seeing the signs of terror in her aunt's eyes, Abigail liked her grandfather even less. "I see," was all she said, knowing that her aunt would only grow more agitated if she were to argue the point. "And you were married to his son?"

Her aunt nodded.

"He has passed on?"

Her aunt nodded again.

"I'm sorry," Abigail said as fresh tears shot to her eyes. "You must have been heart-broken."

Her aunt sighed, "He was a good man."

Watching the woman across from her, Abigail realised that no love had been lost between her aunt and uncle. Although she mourned his death as was expected, she had not loved him. Like so many others, she had married for other reasons.

"Did you have children?" Abigail asked, trying to find a more cheerful subject.

Instantly, her aunt's gaze brightened. "We had a son, who is now married with two children of his own."

"That sounds wonderful. You must be very fond of your grandchildren."

Although a smile came to her lips and she nodded her head, there was a sadness in her aunt's gaze that spoke loud and clear of pain and regret. Something was not as it ought to be in this family. Her family!

Once they arrived at her grandfather's townhouse, a tall and imposing structure, towering over its neighbours, Aunt Mara led her inside. They stopped in the great hall to hand their coats and hats to a footman.

"Welcome back, my lady," an impeccably clad older man with a serious frown addressed them. He was dressed in butler's robes and possessed that air of self-importance only a high-ranking servant did.

"Thank you, Orwel," Aunt Mara replied, her shoulders tense and her voice sounding a tad strained. Apparently, she was not so happy to have returned!

"His grace requests to see Miss Abbott immediately," Orwel continued, "alone."

Aunt Mara swallowed, then forced a smile onto her pale face. "I shall see you at supper," she said to Abigail, gesturing for her to follow in Orwel's wake who had already taken off toward the eastern wing. Quite obviously, her grandfather did not hold her in high regard or his most trusted servant would not have treated her with such open disrespect.

Smiling at her aunt, Abigail hurried after the butler, disliking her grandfather a tad more. Where was this to end?

After walking down a wide hallway, Orwel knocked on a large door, waited for the sign to enter and then stepped forward, not even casting a glance over his shoulder to ensure if his master's granddaughter would follow.

"Your grace, may I present Miss Abbott."

Stepping over the threshold, Abigail was not at all surprised to see that her grandfather's study reminded her of a lion charging a gazelle. Everything in it appeared cold and hostile. Dark curtains hung on the windows, half-drawn even though the day was barely at an end. The wood paneling was dark, matching the floors as well as the enormous desk, separating the duke from the visitors he clearly disliked receiving. On top of everything, the two chairs on the opposite side of the desk looked terribly uncomfortable as though her grandfather had chosen them with great care to discourage people to linger.

With everything Abigail saw, she liked her grandfather a bit less.

"Good day, Miss Abbott," a hoarse voice spoke from the dimness behind the desk. "Welcome to London."

Lifting her gaze, Abigail found her grandfather nod at Orwel, who quit the room immediately. Seated in his large armchair—the only comfortable chair in the room—he merely beckoned her forward, not bothering to rise. His grey eyes slid over her with frank perusal, narrowing slightly as though he disapproved of what he saw.

Abigail suspected few people received his approval.

Determined not to allow him to intimidate her, Abigail squared her shoulders and met his gaze unflinchingly. "Good day, Grandfather. It is so nice to finally meet you."

At her informal address, her grandfather's eyes narrowed, and his lips thinned. Then he inhaled deeply. "You are to address me as *your grace*, do you understand?"

"I shall do my best to remember that, Grandfather." Smiling sweetly, Abigail held his gaze, wondering at the slight twitch in the right corner of his mouth. However, it was gone before she could be certain if it had even been there.

"Do try," he stressed, "for impeccable manners will no doubt aid you in procuring a most suitable match. In addition, I am certain that my name and fortune will assist you in that endeavour."

"A suitable match?" Frowning, Abigail stared at her grandfather.

"Yes, a husband," he clarified, a touch of amusement in his tone. "The season has only just begun, which will give you ample opportunity to get acquainted with suitable gentlemen. I have no doubt that your aunt will be happy to make introductions."

At the self-assured tone in her grandfather's voice, Abigail chuckled, "I can assure you, Grandfather, I am not looking for a husband at present. I..." Swallowing, she forced back tears. "I only just lost my father. I am in no state of mind to—"

"Nonsense!" the duke exclaimed. "You're my granddaughter and you will marry a man of high standing. I shall see to it." He held her gaze, a challenge lighting up his own. "And do try harder." Then he waved his hand in dismissal, and as though he had been eavesdropping on the other side of the door, Orwel stepped in and ushered her outside. "I shall see you to your rooms, Miss."

Somewhat annoyed with her grandfather's commanding demeanour, Abigail followed the old butler. Still, she could not deny that there was something about the duke that spoke to her. At the very least, she felt certain that her stay in London would be far from boring.

And that was exactly what she needed.

Not a husband, to be certain!

But something to take her mind off her father's death and

circumventing her grandfather's orders would certainly prove to be most eventful indeed!

1

THE COLOURS OF A FLOWER

 fortnight later, Abigail had to admit that her grandfather *might possibly* have been correct.

She had indeed found suitors.

A whole flock of them!

And without even trying!

This was worse than she had expected as they seemed determined to pursue her...no matter what she said to discourage them.

While London was a breath-taking city and Abigail enjoyed nothing more but to wander the many streets with her aunt by her side, allowing her eyes to take in all the many wonderful sights, the society she was forced into due to her station was less desirable. And she had to admit she felt a bit disheartened.

"I've already received a marriage proposal!" Abigail exclaimed as she stood on a small pedestal in the modiste's shop, being measured for yet another armada of gowns. "I've only been in town a fortnight, and I've already received a marriage proposal!" Shaking her head, she stared at her aunt.

"Congratulations!" the modiste beamed, clearly missing the touch of panic in Abigail's voice.

Frowning at the dressmaker, Abigail shook her head, then turned her gaze back to her aunt. "Aunt Mara, you need to help me. What do I do? When I refused him, he looked at me as though I had sprouted another head." She inhaled deeply. "And Grandfather was less than amused…although I did get the impression that he wasn't all that fond of Lord What-was-his-name, either."

Aunt Mara sighed, her mouth opening and closing as she considered what to say. Although her aunt was no one to express her thoughts freely, she had come a long way in the past fortnight, obliging her niece wherever she could. It was also possible that Abigail's way of including her aunt in everything she did, sharing her thoughts and asking for advice was slowly wearing the older woman down. However, Abigail could not help but feel that her aunt led a lonely life and that deep down she wished for nothing more than to be needed, included…loved.

"What kind of gentleman are you looking for, my dear?" Aunt Mara tried, knowing full well that Abigail had no intention of accepting any kind of gentleman.

"It's my dowry!" Abigail exclaimed, ignoring her aunt's question. Settling her hands on her hips, she glared at…nothing, but would have if her grandfather had been there. "He did this on purpose to get his way!"

Aunt Mara frowned. "Would you not say it was kind of him to bestow such a large dowry on you? After all, you're a duke's granddaughter, and you deserve no less."

Smiling sweetly at her aunt, Abigail shook her head. "He didn't do it for me…or perhaps only to upset me." A frown drew down her brows as she remembered the sparkle of delight in her grandfather's eyes when she had come home after refusing her first—and luckily, so far her only—marriage proposal, lashing out at him in her dismay, basically ordering him to withdraw her dowry.

All he had done was shaken his head, once again reminding her to address him as *your grace*.

As Abigail had no intention of ever doing so, she had stormed off, not in the least affected by the dark scowl that usually hung on his face. It had only taken a few days for her to realise that her grandfather loved nothing more than to make others tremble in fear. It was his favourite pastime, which he went to great length for.

Oh, she would not tremble! Abigail vowed. At least not with fear! With indignation, most likely! Annoyance, definitely!

Still, the question remained: what was she to do? If this was a game, then her grandfather was winning. And that upset her even more than she liked to admit.

"All right, let's think this over again." Rubbing her temples, Abigail closed her eyes for a moment, forcing all thoughts to focus on the task at hand. "They pursue me because of grandfather's dowry, and he is most unwilling to do anything about that, which means I need to give them another reason to…come to their senses and leave me alone. But how?"

Aunt Mara sighed, a somewhat amused smile on her face. "Oh, dear, there is nothing you could do to discourage them. I assure you it is not merely the dowry his grace bestowed upon you, but your own charms, your kindness and beauty."

"That's it!" Abigail exclaimed, clapping her hands together, before meeting her aunt's rather widened eyes. "My dowry might be a great incentive; however, I doubt London's gentlemen would overlook a potential bride's enormous deficiencies to obtain it."

Aunt Mara frowned, a worried tone in her voice. "What on earth do you mean, Child?"

Laughing, Abigail brushed a curl of her dark hair behind her ear as relief flooded her being. "It's rather simple, I should say. All I have to do is turn myself into an extreme of the worst kind, and they will have no choice but to reconsider sharing their life with a woman as unsuitable as me."

"But you're not unsuitable, my dear. Why would you think that?" Aunt Mara objected. "You're such a beau—"

"Not yet!" Abigail interrupted. "But that can be helped." Then she turned to the modiste, who had been listening to their exchange with rapt attention. "Do you have anything in orange?"

"Orange?" The woman squeaked, casting a careful glance at Aunt Mara. "I beg your pardon, miss, but it…it clashes with your skin tone. A warm r—"

"Exactly!" Abigail said triumphantly, allowing her gaze to sweep across the many accessories displayed in the shop. "Wouldn't an orange gown look lovely with that turquoise shawl over there?"

The looks on the modiste's and her aunt's faces said quite impressively that it would not…which was exactly why Abigail insisted

on purchasing it.

Oh, this was only the beginning! And her grandfather would come to regret the day he had chosen to cross swords with her!

As temperatures began to climb, London's flowers started to awaken from their long sleep, finally able to bask in the warm sun once more and showing off their beautiful colours. As did the ladies of the ton. However, one lady had chosen rather unflattering colours.

Walking into the ballroom with her loyal aunt by her side, Abigail forced herself to suppress the grin that so desperately wanted to show itself to the world. As before, all eyes—or at least most eyes!—turned to her. However, the look in them had changed considerably, and that pleased Abigail greatly as she silently congratulated herself on her ingenious plan. After all, it was working perfectly!

Brushing her hands down her bright yellow gown, a black sash running from one shoulder across her middle to lay gently at her hip, Abigail smiled her brightest smile as though she believed that the crowd that could not help but stare at her thought her the most beautiful creature to ever walk the earth. In truth, Abigail was certain that she resembled a bumble bee!

The only thing that dulled her feelings of euphoria was the rather strained look on her aunt's face. As most people tended to simply overlook her, she had grown accustomed to their inattention and found being in the spotlight a rather uncomfortable experience. Still, she did not abandon her niece, and Abigail was truly grateful to her.

Strolling over to the refreshment table, Abigail helped herself to a glass of lemonade, handing another one to her aunt. Then they strolled through Lord Passmore's large townhouse, nodding their heads at acquaintances left and right. Although people returned their greeting, few dared approach, and when one gentleman with a rather glassy look to his eyes finally did, he was rewarded with a glass of lemonade spilled down his front.

"Oh, my lord, look what you did!" Abigail exclaimed in a rather high-pitched voice, loud enough for all to hear, pretending she had had no hand in the poor man's-soaked shirt. "You ought to watch your step and perhaps try to refrain from indulging in Lord Passmore's spirits."

Gasps echoed to her ears at her frank reprimand of an earl of the ton. Still, Abigail could not deny that she delighted in these little games!

Mumbling an apology, Aunt Mara drew her aside. "Please, think this through, Child. If you continue to antagonise these people, you will be left all alone. Is that what you want?"

Abigail sighed, knowing that her aunt meant well. "What I want is not to be married off to a man who could not care less about who I am."

"But this is not who you are!" her aunt insisted.

Abigail shrugged. "Maybe a little. Still, no gentleman has ever tried to find out more about me besides the amount of my dowry."

Aunt Mara shook her head. "Would you if it were reversed? Would you wish to get to know a gentleman who spilled his drink on you? Who stepped on your toes while dancing and then accused you of stepping on his? Who knocks down a priceless antique without even apologising and then blames you for placing it in an inconvenient spot?" Again, she shook her head at Abigail. "I should think not."

Abigail laughed, "You know me too well, dear Aunt. However, at present, I have no wish to get better acquainted with the gentlemen of the ton." She swallowed, and her voice sobered as grief fought its way out into the open. "I've only just lost my father, and I cannot see myself opening my heart to anyone right now." Looking at her aunt with pleading eyes, Abigail grasped the older woman's hands. "But these little games take my mind off the sadness and loss, and for a short while, they make me smile. Is that truly so bad?"

Aunt Mara sighed, then gently patted Abigail's hand. "Of course not, Dear. You have a kind heart, and you do deserve true happiness. All I am worried about is that you might one day find yourself wishing for a husband, only to find that your reputation is standing in the way of a happy union. After all, people are already calling y–" Clasping her mouth shut, Aunt Mara averted her gaze, a tinge of red coming to her pale cheeks.

Abigail chuckled, "You need not worry, Aunt. I am aware what people call me." She smiled at the shocked expression on her aunt's face and squared her shoulders to pronounce proudly, "The most awful woman in all of England!"

"You know this?" Aunt Mara gasped, wringing her hands nervously. "I'm sorry. I–"

"Don't be," Abigail interrupted. "After all, I've worked hard for my reputation. Do you think it's easy to speak with this shrill tone in

my voice? Or to step on my dance partner's toes? Not at all. It requires great precision. Not everyone could do it." Smiling encouragingly, Abigail drew one of her aunt's hands into hers. "Do not worry, Aunt Mara. I know what I'm doing, and I want you to know that I'm enjoying myself quite profusely. The added side effect is that I haven't received a single marriage proposal in over a fortnight." Drawing her aunt's arm through the crook of her own, she pulled her toward the refreshment table. "Come, let's drink to this." A chuckle rose from her throat. "I promise I shall do my utmost not to spill my drink on you."

Aunt Mara rolled her eyes at her niece. However, Abigail delighted in the soft smile that came to the older woman's lips. "You'll be the death of me, my dear."

"Oh, I love you, too, Aunt Mara," Abigail trilled, knowing how fortunate she was that her grandfather had sent for her. Otherwise, she would have been all alone in the world. And it felt so good to be loved.

2

THE MOST AWFUL WOMAN IN ALL OF ENGLAND

ith his sister happily married to his oldest friend, Griffin Radley, Earl of Amberly, had begun to feel like a third wheel. Although he considered both his closest confidantes, the dynamic in their relationship had changed. Now, Winifred and Trent only had eyes for each other, and although Griffin was happy to see them so…well, happy, he could not help but envy the bond between them. Was it time for him to find a wife?

The thought had occurred to him ever since his little sister had decided she was getting old and would need to find a husband fast if she wanted to be a mother. Fortunately, he had been able to sway her from her path of obtaining a husband through her rather practical approach and lead her into the arms of the man she had loved all her life. Still, their happily-ever-after had come at a price…for Griffin!

To have a say in her choice, Griffin had to enter into a pact with his rational-minded sister, giving her an equal say when it came to finding the right woman for him. And now that Winifred was happily

married, she loved nothing better than to remind him of that fact and tease him endlessly. He would have thought she'd be grateful for his interference as it had led to a most fortunate outcome of this whole husband-hunting nonsense. Still, Winifred had a bit of a wicked side to her, and he did not think she would stop teasing him any time soon.

While chatting with a couple of friends, Griffin glanced across the room at the dance floor where his sister and her new husband twirled around to the notes of yet another waltz. Although they seemed to be arguing about…something—as they commonly did—their eyes glowed with devotion, and Griffin could not deny a deep sense of satisfaction at having been instrumental in seeing his sister happily married.

"They look happy," his friend Lord Berenton commented, his bushy eyebrows going up and down like a caterpillar crawling over his face. "Still," he chuckled, a teasing gleam in his eyes, "I cannot help but be cross with you for giving them your blessing. Have I not told you time and time again that she was the one for me?"

Griffin laughed, "I assure you I only gave them my blessing to protect you. My sister has a way of pushing people over the edge, and I'm afraid to say this, but you are no match for her."

Berenton's bushy eyebrows drew down. "Do you think so poorly of me?"

"Not at all, old friend. But I know my sister too well. Believe me, the day they got married was your lucky day."

"You sound a tad relieved." Squinting his eyes, Berenton watched him. "Do you not miss her company?"

Griffin sighed. *Terribly.*

However, before he could answer, the happy couple came walking toward them, joining their little circle. Instantly, Berenton turned to Winifred, and Griffin tried to roll his eyes at him quietly. "My congratulations on your wedding. From what Amberly told me he is quite relieved to have his sister well married." Turning to Griffin, Berenton grinned at him. "I cannot understand why you had trouble marrying her off. A beauty like her."

Griffin sighed. *If only you knew!* Remembering the many sleepless nights and stressful days when he had tried his best to prove to his sister that love was the best reason to choose a husband, only to have her *rational* mind thwart him time and time again, Griffin still could not help but feel exhausted. Maybe he should repay the favour and tease her as much as she always delighted in teasing him.

Grinning at her, Griffin told his friend, "Mind you, she had no lack of suitors. However, I'm afraid my sister was quite particular about the kind of husband she had in mind. I tell you it caused me many sleepless nights."

Everyone laughed, and more than one friend patted him on the shoulder as though he had just crossed the African desert and made it through alive.

As expected, payback was not far off.

Turning to her brother, Winifred smiled at him sweetly. Still, having known her all his life, Griffin had no trouble detecting the touch of mischief that had come to her eyes. "I suppose that it is now my turn to find my brother a suitable bride."

Unable to keep his stomach from twisting into knots, Griffin took a deep breath as laughter echoed around him. Deep down, he had to admit he was waiting for the day she would finally make good on her threat! Would today be the day?

Perhaps it was the suspense that was killing him.

Although he had no doubt that his sister loved him, he also knew her tendency to rationalise emotions. What if she found him a bride she truly believed to be his perfect match? And what if said bride did not appeal to him at all? Would his sister insist, thinking she knew better? Thinking he would eventually come around? Or would she show mercy?

As though he had read Griffin's thoughts, Berenton declared with utter delight. "You're at her mercy now, Amberly!" Then he turned smiling eyes to Winifred, and Griffin felt as though he was going to be sick. "My lady, if you require any assistance, do not hesitate to call on me. I'm quite familiar with a number of eligible ladies and could point you in the right direction."

"How kind of you, my lord," Winifred trilled in that voice that meant she was up to no good.

"In fact, there are many eligible ladies here tonight," Berenton continued, completely unimpressed by the threatening glares Griffin shot him. "However, I would advise against Miss Abbott." He leaned closer into the group and whispered, "She's rumoured to be the most awful woman in all of England."

Griffin almost groaned at the intrigued look that came to his sister's gaze, and he knew that he was doomed. Still, shock had his eyes popping open and his jaw dropping down. "Oh, no, you wouldn't," he stammered, aware that no matter what he did his sister's mind was already made up.

Smiling sweetly, Winifred met his gaze. "You gave me your word, dear brother, and besides what's fair is fair." Then she turned to Berenton. "Would you be so kind as to point out Miss Abbott to me?"

Berenton's face lit up with delight, and he winked at Griffin. "I most certainly would."

Groaning, Griffin forced a deep breath into his lungs, glaring at Berenton as he escorted Winifred across the room. *Very well! This was a friend he could certainly do without!*

"Do you know who this Miss Abbott is?" Trent asked beside him as everyone's gaze remained fixed on Berenton and Winifred, trying to catch a glimpse of London's most eligible shrew!

"I do not," Griffin forced out through gritted teeth, feeling his pulse hammering in his neck. Suddenly, his collar seemed much too tight for comfort, reminding him of a hangman's noose!

With many couples occupying the dance floor and blocking their view, Griffin had to crane his neck. His gaze swept over several good-looking young ladies before he saw Berenton stop to introduce Winifred to…

Griffin's mouth fell open. "She cannot be serious?"

Trent cleared his throat, the expression on his face speaking of a similar disbelief. "One should think so. However, knowing your sister, I'm afraid you're out of luck, my friend."

Feeling the blood in his veins turn to ice, Griffin stared as his sister smiled friendly at a young woman in a painfully bright pink gown with orange blossoms, her dark hair pulled back into a tight bun, making her face appear as though it was stretched to its limits. Even from across the room, he could hear her shrill laugh as she returned his sister's greeting, her hands gesturing wildly and—inevitably—smacking Lord Stockdale on the side of the face.

Surprised, the young gentleman held a hand to his cheek, looking rather taken aback at the young woman beside him. Miss Abbott, however, did not seem to see any fault in her actions for the look on her face did not speak of an offered apology, but a reprimand instead.

"She can't be serious," Griffin whispered, all air leaving his body as his future loomed threateningly on the horizon. "She wouldn't be that cruel, would she?" Forcing his gaze away, Griffin stared at

Trent. "Did I do anything to make her angry? Is she mad at me? I mean, did I not do everything in my power to see her happy? I found her perfect match after all."

Trent smiled at the compliment. "Don't take this too seriously. You know your sister. You know how she loves to tease. Simply play along…and this'll all go away…eventually."

Griffin drew in a deep breath, squaring his shoulders as he watched his sister speak to Miss Abbott. This woman was impossible, and yet, Winifred acted as though she had met an old friend, leaning in conspiratorially and whispering something Griffin did not doubt would lead to his doom.

After a small eternity, Winifred finally took her leave and made her way back across the large room, stopping here and there to exchange a quick word with one of their host's guests. "She is doing this solely to torture me," Griffin growled, willing himself to hate his sister with every fibre of his being…and still failing miserably.

Trent laughed, "I suppose that's fairly obvious."

When Winifred and Berenton finally reached them, Griffin was close to exploding. "You cannot be serious," he snapped for what seemed like the millionth time that night, his disbelief stretched too thin.

Winifred frowned in confusion. Still, the soft twitch of her upper lip did not escape Griffin's attention. "What do you mean? She's such a lovely lady, but gravely misunderstood." She sighed, glancing over her shoulder at Miss Abbott, who in that very moment spilled her drink on yet another unfortunate gentleman who had dared to come near her. "What do you have against her?" Winifred enquired innocently, batting her eyelashes.

In that moment, Griffin wanted to strangle her. Still, all he could do was open and close his mouth a couple of times before his mind was back in order and supplied him with what to say. "I don't even know where to begin," he stammered, his pulse hitching higher with each moment. "That woman is impossible. Look at her! You cannot be serious." Shaking his head, he frowned at the sister he had known all his life. "What do you have against me? I'm your brother, remember? I thought you cared about me."

Laughing softly, Winifred placed a gentle hand on his arm. "Do not worry, dear brother. Yes, I do love you, and I would never do anything to make you miserable. Trust me. I know what I'm doing."

Griffin could only hope so.

Sighing, Winifred turned to her husband. "Poor Miss Abbott is still fairly new in town. I believe I shall call on her and see that she is settled in and not lacking company." Out of the corner of her eye, she glanced at Griffin. "Who knows, soon we might be the best of friends!"

As Trent led his wife back to the dance floor, casting an apologetic glance over his shoulder at his old friend, Griffin gritted his teeth to the point that he thought they would splinter in his mouth.

"Not having a good day, are we?" Berenton observed beside him, a touch of suppressed humour in his voice, and clasped a hand on Griffin's shoulder. "Should we get drunk?"

Griffin sighed. That sounded like as good a plan as any.

After all, he had learnt long ago that he was no match for his sister's devious mind. All he could do was hope that she hadn't forgotten that she loved him.

She would not truly suggest he marry Miss Abbot, would she?

SOMETHING RATHER UNEXPECTED

randfather, I need to speak with you!" Not bothering to knock, Abigail burst into the duke's study, pleased to see his head jerk up and his eyes settle on her with a hint of annoyance.

Merely a hint? That was progress! Abigail thought.

"Your grace," her grandfather reminded her, leaning back in his leather armchair, the scowl on his face daring her to ignore him.

Which, of course, was a challenge Abigail could not help but accept. "Certainly, Grandfather."

Rolling his eyes at her, he gestured to the chair opposite his large desk. "What can I do for you this morning?"

Settling onto the chair, Abigail frowned as she scooted left and right, trying to get comfortable. When all her attempts failed, she looked up at her grandfather, a hint of annoyance in her eyes. "You don't want people to stay long," she accused, her lips curling up in amusement. "These chairs are uncomfortable for a reason, are they not?"

The hint of a smile flashed over her grandfather's weathered face, and she thought to detect an almost imperceptible nod of his head. "Is this all you came to say?"

Abigail sighed, "Not at all." Meeting her grandfather's gaze openly, she leaned forward in confidence. "Before I can say anything at all, I need your word that what I'm about to tell you will remain between the two of us. Do you promise?"

A deep frown drew down her grandfather's brows. "I will do no such thing."

"Grandfather!" Abigail chided. "This is important. It's about Aunt Mara."

A scoff escaped his lips, "Then it's not important at all."

Shocked by his cold words, Abigail rose to her feet, her gaze not wavering from his. Then she stepped toward his massive desk and leaned down, resting her hands on the smooth surface. "She respects you greatly. She does whatever you ask of her without ever—"

"She's my son's widow," her grandfather snapped. "It's her duty to—"

"You owe her—"

"I owe her nothing!" he retorted, a touch of red crawling up his neck as he stared at his granddaughter, indignation at her forward behaviour all too visible in his grey eyes. "She knows her place, as should you."

Inhaling a deep breath, Abigail knew what was expected of her, and yet, she could not back down and bow her head.

Raised far away from London society and its rules, Abigail had never been taught to be subservient to titled families, to see them as her betters, to believe that they deserved more than she did. No, indeed, her father had taught her that people were born equals and that one could only set oneself apart by doing what was right and fair and just...not by what was easy.

After everything Aunt Mara had done for her, she deserved Abigail's loyalty, her support, her strength. She had welcomed her into the family and—more importantly—into her heart, easing the pain of her father's passing with her kind words and gentle reminders that he would have wanted her to be happy.

"I know very well where my place is, *Grandfather*," Abigail said, her own grey eyes resting on his, her voice not disrespectful but determined nonetheless. "Do you?"

31

His jaw tensed as he stared at her, momentarily taken aback, and she could see that he was at a loss. Never in his life had people dared to speak to him thus.

"I came here," Abigail began as she straightened, lifting her hands off the desk, "to ask about her son, her grandchildren. She seems to miss them terribly, but she never sees them. Never even speaks of them." Shaking her head to emphasise her confusion, Abigail sank back into her chair, wincing slightly when the hard wood cut into her back. "What happened? She always looks so miserable."

For a long moment, her grandfather's gaze remained on her before he drew in a slow breath, his eyes moving with the indecision she knew he felt. Did people in his family never speak of how they felt? What they loved? Feared? Hoped for? "My son died almost a decade ago," he finally said, his voice low, quiet, almost imperceptible. "However, I do not believe it affected her much." A grim tone had come to his voice.

Abigail frowned. "They did not love each other."

The duke shook his head. "I suppose not." He swallowed. "She did as any widow is expected to, but I never saw deep sorrow in her."

"Can you blame her?" At her words, her grandfather's head snapped up, and he stared at her with shock. "I don't mean to speak ill of your son, but from what I've learnt of marriages among the upper class, there is very little emotion involved. How do you expect her to mourn someone she never cared for?"

Her grandfather's lips thinned, but he did not question her reasoning.

"What about her son? Your grandson? Are they not close?"

"They were. Once." Meeting her gaze, the duke crossed his arms in front of his chest, and Abigail could see the reluctance to speak about such personal matters in the way he held himself rigid as though he was the one sitting in the tortuously uncomfortable chair. "When Everett made his intention known of proposing to Lord Simwell's daughter, his mother counselled him to reconsider. Apparently, she did not believe they were a good match."

"And she was right, wasn't she?"

Her grandfather nodded. "Theirs was never a happy marriage. At least not after the first year. I suppose my grandson's wife found out about his mother's objections. Ever since, they've become estranged and she's been doing her utmost to keep the children away from their grandmother."

Abigail sighed, finally understanding the loneliness and regret that filled Aunt Mara's life. "Have you never tried to help her? To smooth things between her and her son as well as her daughter-in-law?"

"It was not my place," her grandfather bit out.

"Not your place?" Abigail echoed. "You're a family. He's your grandson. They're your great-grandchildren. It most certainly is your place." Inhaling deeply, Abigail tried to calm her rattled nerves. Never in her life had she heard such nonsense. "What do we do?"

"What do you mean?"

Rolling her eyes, Abigail once more stepped toward his desk. "Grandfather, I can see that all of you have been a little out of practice but let me tell you how family works." A teasing curl came to her lips as she looked at him, trying to break the ice that had frosted over her family's hearts for too long. "When one of us is miserable, so are the others because we care about each other. And even though you will probably never admit to it, you know that I'm right. We need to help her. Any suggestions?"

As her grandfather stared at her a bit open-mouthed, a sharp knock came on the door. "Enter," the duke croaked, then cleared his throat as he forced the mask of detachedness back on his face before Orwel entered.

"I apologise for the intrusion, your grace," he said, giving a slight bow before his gaze momentarily shifted to Abigail, "but there's a Lady Chadwick here to see Miss Abbott."

Taken aback, Abigail blinked. Lady Chadwick? Was that the young woman who had spoken to her the other day at the ball? She had certainly been kind, surprised Abigail by even addressing her, but Abigail would never have thought that she truly meant to call on her. Few people meant what they said.

"Do you intend to let her wait all day?" her grandfather asked, a teasing tone in his voice now that the focus had shifted back to her. "The ton might not look on that with kind eyes."

Abigail snorted, "Quite frankly, I couldn't care less about what the ton does or doesn't do." Then she turned on her heel and headed for the door. However, with her hand on the handle she stopped and turned back to look at her grandfather. "Perhaps you should speak with your grandson. He might be able to find a way to smooth things between his wife and his mother."

Her grandfather scoffed, "At this point, I do not believe he cares."

Fed up with her family, Abigail heaved a deep sigh. "Then make him care," she snapped, then rushed out the door before her grandfather could object.

Trying to put her family's issues out of her mind, Abigail wondered what had brought Lady Chadwick over that morning. After all, never had any lady sought Abigail's company for her devious plan to drive away all eligible bachelors had also succeeded nicely in convincing the ladies of the ton that she was not good company and they did not wish to be seen with her.

Her reputation had indeed suffered. Unfortunately, a few gentlemen still insisted on pursuing her. Only friends she had none.

As Abigail walked by the large mirror in the front hall on her way to the drawing room, she caught sight of her reflection and realised with a start that she had not bothered to dress in her usual hideous fashion that morning.

But why would she have? After all, she had not expected any visitors today. Her hair was gathered in the back and pinned up gently while some tendrils danced down from her temples, and she wore a simple pale-yellow dress, quite unlike the one that made her look like a bumblebee.

Well, it could not be helped, and besides, she was not receiving an eligible bachelor bent on procuring her hand, now was she?

Drawing in a deep breath, Abigail had to admit she was a tad nervous. Never had she found herself craving the good opinion of a lady of the ton, and she realised how much she wished for a friend.

Stepping into the room, Abigail found the young woman admiring a watercolour hanging on the wall by the pianoforte. "Good morning, Lady Chadwick," she greeted her, trying to still her trembling hands. "How nice of you to call on me."

"The pleasure is all mine," Lady Chadwick replied, her eyes aglow and a genuine smile decorating her lovely features. Instantly, Abigail felt herself relax.

"Would you care for some tea?" she asked, already ringing the bell.

"That sounds wonderful," her visitor replied. "It's still a bit chilly outside."

Gesturing for Lady Chadwick to take a seat, Abigail chose a spot across from her. Deciding there was no use in dancing around the bush, she asked, "What brings you here?"

An amused smile spread over her guest's face as she leaned forward as though wishing to share a secret. "I've come to be your friend."

Abigail could not keep her jaw from dropping just a tad. "My friend?" she echoed, wondering if the young lady across from her had the ability to read minds. "Quite frankly, I've rarely had someone speak to me so…"

"Bluntly?" Lady Chadwick offered. "Well, I find being honest about one's intentions saves time."

Abigail laughed, "I suppose it does. May I then ask what made you want to be my friend? I admit I'm rather surprised."

Lady Chadwick shrugged. "For one, I know you to be new in town and as I find myself in a similar position, I thought we might be a good fit."

"You're new in town?"

Lady Chadwick nodded. "My brother and I only returned from the continent a few months ago. We'd been away from England for about five years, and we're only just getting reacquainted with society."

Abigail nodded, feeling excitement rise in her chest. Would she truly have a friend by the end of the day? "May I enquire if there were other reasons?"

A slight blush came to Lady Chadwick's face as she tried to control the large smile that threatened to draw up the corners of her mouth. "Well, quite frankly, my brother has always accused me of being too rational-minded, and I admit lately I've come to realise that he might not have been…completely wrong."

Abigail laughed.

"Well, to make it short, when I saw you at the ball, I was intrigued and decided to follow an impulse. I don't try to make a habit out of it, but I suppose there is no harm in doing it occasionally."

Again, Abigail laughed, realising that she liked Lady Chadwick quite a bit. The young woman had a refreshingly open way of speaking her mind as well as a sense of humour that spoke to Abigail. "You were intrigued?"

Lady Chadwick nodded. "I mean no offence, but you looked quite…odd that night." Her gaze held Abigail's for a moment before she continued. "That hideous dress and your hair pulled back so tightly I swear I felt my own scalp tingle. I couldn't help but wonder why a young woman would do such a thing and thought to myself that a

remarkable mind and fascinating character were most likely at its root."
She shrugged, a questioning smile curling up her lips.

Not having expected such a compliment as well as the depth of
her guest's observation, Abigail could not deny that it pleased her
nonetheless. After all, despite the open disapproval she saw at every ball
when people regarded her appearance, they never dared say so to her
face. Instead, they tried to find one way or other to give her a
compliment whenever they found themselves put on the spot. "You're
here to enquire about my reason for dressing so...oddly?"

Lady Chadwick laughed, her gaze gliding over Abigail's
appearance. "Well, quite frankly, today you do look a lot more like
yourself. So, there must be a reason? Isn't there always?"

Abigail inhaled a deep breath. Although she wished to share her
motivation with Lady Chadwick, she knew she ought to be cautions.
After all, what did she truly know about her? "You're quite right, my
lady. I certainly do have a reason, however, I find that—"

"You're not quite ready to share it with a stranger?" Lady
Chadwick chuckled good-naturedly. "That's quite all right. Well, then
tell me what has brought you to town. I was told that you're his grace's
granddaughter."

Abigail swallowed, not fond to retell the story of her father's
passing. However, to her great relief, she soon saw honest sympathy in
Lady Chadwick's gaze, who reciprocated by telling her of losing her
own parents in a carriage accident five years ago. Their loss had
upended her life as much as losing her father had changed Abigail's.
While she had come to London to stay with her grandfather, Lady
Chadwick and her brother had travelled the world, trying their best to
find a way to cope with the loss while remembering that life continued
and that feeling happy was no reason for feeling guilty as well.

Over the course of the next fortnight, Abigail spent many
wonderful days in Lady Chadwick's company, delighting in their new-
found friendship. They had a lot in common and discovered more
every day. Most days Abigail walked around with a deep smile on her
face, noticing that Aunt Mara delighted in seeing her so happy. In
consequence, Abigail continued to prod her grandfather, urging him to
speak to his grandson.

So far, he was resisting, but Abigail had no doubt that he would
eventually admit defeat. Perhaps not as straightforward as saying it out
loud. He would most likely conjure ridiculous excuse; however, the
result would be the same.

"And she never sees them?" Winifred asked one afternoon as they walked around the new conservatory her husband had added to their townhouse. "How sad!"

Abigail nodded. "She tries not to show it, but whenever we go through the park and she sees children their age, her eyes tear up." Sighing, Abigail shook her head. "I wish I could help her, but my grandfather is currently less than willing."

Winifred laughed, "I'm certain you will convince him before too long."

"I do hope so," Abigail exclaimed, wondering if she ought to speak to her cousin herself.

"Ah, there you are!"

Turning toward the voice, Abigail found two men walking into the conservatory, their faces cheerful as they seemed to be in conversation with one another. One of the two men was Winifred's husband, Lord Chadwick, whom Abigail had met once or twice while visiting her friend. The other, however, she could not recall ever having met.

Strangely enough though, when his gaze came to rest on her, the smile slid off his face as though she had just insulted him, and his eyes took on a hard expression as he turned to his sister, open accusation in the way he looked at her.

At a loss, Abigail turned to her friend, who ignored the young man's glare and gestured for the two of them to enter. "Abigail," she began, smiling at her with a strange new glow in her eyes, "you remember my husband, Lord Chadwick. And this is my brother Lord Amberly. Brother, may I introduce you to Miss Abbott."

Abigail swallowed as the young man stepped forward and then inclined his head to her, the look on his face one of utter displeasure—quite in contrast to the words that followed. "Miss Abbott, it is a pleasure to make your acquaintance."

"It is indeed, my lord," Abigail replied without thinking, still trying to understand what was happening. Quite obviously, something was very much amiss! She could have sworn if it had not been for her presence, Lord Amberly would have lashed out at his sister for…something.

Winifred in turn raised her eyebrows at him…almost triumphantly while her husband tried his best to suppress a smile.

As though lighting struck her in that moment, Abigail suddenly understood with perfect clarity what was going on! Her new friend, whom she had come to trust, whom she had almost shared her secret with, had lied to her for Winifred's own motivation for seeking her out now seemed quite clear.

To introduce Abigail to her brother. To persuade her to accept his proposal when it came. To forward her own agenda of seeing her brother well settled.

Lord Amberly, on the other hand, seemed more than a bit reluctant to pursue her. Indeed, he kept a safe distance, barely even looking at her, as though she had the plague.

Quite obviously, brother and sister were of opposite minds regarding whom he ought to marry.

"I'm afraid I must take my leave," Abigail said, lifting her chin defiantly, unwilling to reveal how much Winifred's—Lady Chadwick's!—betrayal hurt her. "My aunt is expecting me." Then, without another word and ignoring her hostess's pleas for her to stay, Abigail rushed from the room, gathered her coat, shawl and hat from the footman in the foyer and left without a look back.

Stepping out onto the street, she sighed, her heart aching with the loss of a friend she had come to care for.

Alone once more.

4

TRUST GIVEN & RECEIVED

The moment he heard the front door close, Griffin felt himself explode.

"How dare you!" he growled, glaring at his sister with never felt outrage. "Have I not made it clear that I have no interest in Miss Abbott whatsoever? She is not the kind of woman I wish to marry, and I demand that you respect that!" Gritting his teeth against the string of words that threatened to spill from his mouth—words he had never thought he would say in his sister's presence, let alone *to* her!—Griffin silently counted to ten, clenching and unclenching his fists, hoping to relieve some of the anger that surged through his veins.

"You demand?" Gawking at him, Winifred shook her head, clearly oblivious to the rage that held him in its clutches. "Do you remember what you promised me, dear brother? Or shall I help you refresh your memory?"

"I know very well what I promised you!" Griffin hissed, casting a glance at his friend, who stood silent as a pillar of salt, observing the siblings' exchange with rapt attention. "However, I doubt that *you* do. I never forced you to socialise with a man you disliked. Why would you force Miss Abbott on me when I've made it unmistakably clear that—no matter what!—I will not marry her?"

Chuckling as though all of this was terribly amusing misunderstanding, Winifred stepped forward, her gaze focusing on his, and he got the distinct feeling that she was about to catch him in a lie. "Are you certain?" she asked, a clear challenge in her dark brown eyes.

Griffin swallowed, wrecking his brain. Was he? "Of course, I am."

Shaking her head in what he assumed to be disbelief, Winifred laughed. "Your memory is faulty indeed, dear brother. Well, then allow me to enlighten you because you did force on me the company of a man I disliked. Not even you can deny that?"

Frowning, Griffin stared at her, unable to make sense of what she was saying. "How can you say that? Lord Haverton was a perfect gentleman in every regard, and you cannot deny that you liked him."

Winifred shrugged. "I do not deny it."

A low growl rose from Trent's throat, and Winifred glanced at him, a teasing smile coming to her lips.

"Then who do you speak of?" Griffin demanded, feeling his pulse speed up once more. "After all, he's the only gentleman you spent a considerable amount of time with. Yes, I made other suggestions here and there, but they never led anywhere, and I never forced you to pursue them, did I?"

"You did not. At least not with these gentlemen."

"Then who?" Griffin snapped, raking his fingers through his hair. "Who on earth do you speak of?"

Her brows drew down into a frown as a soft chuckle escaped her. "You really don't understand, do you?" Then she glanced at her husband, whose gaze grew dark as though promising retribution. But for what?

"I'm talking about my husband," Winifred finally said, a touch of annoyance in her voice.

Griffin's eyes bulged. "What? You cannot be serious? I never—"

"Yes, you did," she insisted, her hands on her hips and her eyes narrowed into slits. "I told you that I disliked his company—"

"But—"

"No! I did, didn't I?" Winifred demanded.

Gritting his teeth, Griffin nodded.

"And still, you kept forcing him on me—"

Trent chuckled, but a dark glare from his wife shut him up

instantly.

"Don't even for a moment believe that I didn't see what you were doing, leaving us alone together, always coming up with these last-minute excuses for why you couldn't stay." Her lips twisted into an angry snarl. "Do you have any idea how angry I was with you for that? Did you even notice?"

"But you liked him!" Griffin insisted, unable to understand what his sister was saying. "You even loved him." Shaking his head, he pointed at his best friend. "You married him! How can you say—?"

"I told you I did not want to see him, didn't I?" his sister demanded, growing more annoyed when he stared at her blankly. "Didn't I?"

"Yes, you did, but—"

"No but!" Winifred snapped before she drew in a slow breath and her features began to soften, her voice calm again. "I told you then just as you are telling me now. And just like you, I feel as though I see something you don't seem to be aware of." She nodded. "Yes, you were right. I loved Trent, and I'm glad you did what you did." Stepping forward, she took his hand in hers, her soft eyes looking into his, asking him to trust her. "Now, let me do the same for you."

"But I don't love her," Griffin objected, wondering what his sister had seen that had eluded him.

Winifred scoffed, "Of course not, how could you? You've barely spoken a word to her." Sighing, she squeezed his hand. "I'm not asking you to go and ask for her hand right now. All I'm saying is that I want you to give her a chance. She is not the woman you think she is, and I truly believe that you would be a good match for each other." A soft smile curled up the corners of her mouth. "As much as I love teasing you, I would never jeopardise your happiness. I can only hope you know that."

Griffin nodded, remembering when their roles had been reversed, when he had asked her to trust him, promising that he would do what he could to ensure that she would not end up with the wrong man. Fortunately, she had not. But what about him? Could his sister be right? What had she seen in Miss Abbott that would make her believe that they would be a good match?

"I admit that night at the ball," Winifred continued, "when I asked to be introduced to Miss Abbott, I wanted to see you squirm." The left corner of her mouth twitched. "But that is all. I would never make you unhappy. I would never want you to be with someone who would make you unhappy."

"I know," Griffin whispered, pulling his sister into a warm embrace. "I know you wouldn't." Stepping back, he looked into her eyes, drawing a slow and somewhat agonising breath into his lungs. "Fine. I trust you. I will give her a chance."

"That's all I ask."

Griffin nodded, hoping that that was true.

5

HONEST WORDS

Alone, Abigail stood in the corner of the room, gazing at the dancing couples.

Well, not alone. Aunt Mara was with her.

Still, Abigail had hoped to spend some of her time with her new friend. Someone her own age. Someone who would understand in ways Aunt Mara could not. Someone she could confide in.

Well, that someone had not been Winif–Lady Chadwick.

Swallowing, Abigail brushed her hands over her dark purple gown, laced with brown ornaments, giving it a mud brown impression. Again, the modiste had flinched at her choice, and again, Abigail had insisted. After all, her plan seemed to be working more perfectly every day.

Where her dance card had been bursting full in the beginning, it now had gaping holes, forcing on her many moments of inactivity. Moments in which Abigail wished she had a friend to talk to and laugh with.

Well, that seemed to be a hollow dream.

At least, at present.

"Smile, my dear," Aunt Mara encouraged, a gentle smile on her kind features. "You're far too young for worry lines. Look, there's Lady Chadwick with her husband. That ought to put a smile on your face."

Abigail swallowed as her gaze involuntarily shifted to the beautiful young woman in a stunning dress, walking into the ballroom on her husband's arm. She looked happy. Truly happy!

Abigail sighed, realising that despite her own insistence to the contrary, she envied Winif—Lady Chadwick. What would it feel like to—?

Lady Chadwick's gaze met hers, and her warm brown eyes seemed to light up. A soft smile drew up the corners of her mouth, and after leaning closer to her husband to whisper something to him, she released his arm and hastened toward Abigail.

Swallowing a lump in her throat, Abigail wished she could simply run from the room.

"Good evening, Abigail," Lady Chadwick greeted her, a warm smile on her face as her gaze shifted from her to her aunt. "Good evening, Lady Bradish. It is truly wonderful to see you here."

As Aunt Mara returned the kind greeting, casting a questioning gaze at her niece, Abigail took the moment to square her shoulders and lift her chin a fraction. No matter what, she would not beg for Lady Chadwick's friendship...even if she began to feel the loneliness that threatened her heart.

"May I speak to you for a moment?" Lady Chadwick asked, her eyes pleading, and Abigail felt herself nod in agreement before she had even made up her mind.

"I shall see if they have any lemonade," Aunt Mara mumbled, squeezing Abigail's hand before she walked away.

"I feel the need to apologise," Lady Chadwick began once they were alone, "although I have to admit I do not know why."

As her head whipped around, Abigail stared at the other woman. "You cannot mean that."

Lady Chadwick shrugged, an apologetic smile on her face. "I saw how upset you were the day you met my brother—I can only assume it was him because you'd met my husband before—however, I do not know why. From what he said, I do not believe the two of you are acquainted so I cannot understand how meeting him could have upset you thus."

Abigail stared at her former friend, wondering if the honest confusion she saw on Lady Chadwick's face was genuine. Or was she

44

simply a good actress? "Why did you introduce me to him?" Abigail asked, her voice faint as though a part of her was afraid of the answer.

Lady Chadwick shrugged as though that ought to be obvious. "Because I thought you would suit each other. Because you are both important to me, and I wanted you to get to know one another."

Abigail could not deny the surge of joy that swept through her body. Still, could she trust it? Could she trust Lady Chadwick's words? "Why did you speak to me that night at the ball? Why did you ask to be introduced?"

Lady Chadwick frowned. "I already told you that."

"But was it the truth?"

Lady Chadwick's frown deepened, a touch of concern in her warm eyes. "Of course, it was. Do you have any reason not to believe me?" Her gaze searched Abigail's face. "Why do *you* think I spoke to you? Why do *you* think I introduced you to my brother?"

Abigail swallowed, then opened her mouth before she had even made up her mind how to reply. However, that was as far as she got for Lady Chadwick's mouth suddenly fell open and her eyes widened as sudden realisation showed on her face. "That's why you dress like this!" she exclaimed, quickly lowering her voice as a head or two turned in their direction.

Abigail froze, unable to resist as her friend pulled her aside.

"This is an act, is it not?" Lady Chadwick asked, her gaze seeking Abigail's. "You hope to drive away your suitors, but why? Do you not wish to marry?"

Abigail drew in a deep breath as the need to share her worries grew in her chest. "I do. Perhaps not so soon after my father's death when I hardly know my own heart. But in general, yes, I do."

"Then why−?"

"Because I do not want a man who merely seeks my dowry," Abigail hissed under her breath. "The moment the size of my dowry became known, men flocked to me as though I were a siren." She scoffed, shaking her head. "I wager my grandfather only did this to rid himself of me. He doesn't care about me. Why would he? He never even cared about my mother." Feeling tears sting behind her eyes, Abigail turned her head away, blinking her lashes rapidly to dispel them.

Following, Lady Chadwick sighed, "I admit the ton is mostly persuaded into marriage by superficial attributes," she said, a hint of bitterness in her tone as though she despised that truth as much as

Abigail did. "However," she grasped Abigail's hand, "I did not single you out because of your dowry. You have my word on that, and I hope that you can believe it."

Abigail swallowed. "Then why?"

Lady Chadwick smiled. "Did I not tell you already?"

"You did. Still, I—"

"It's the truth," Lady Chadwick insisted. "Although I admit that my brother is currently unable to see past your masquerade," a soft chuckle escaped her, "I do believe that once he does, he will care for you."

Abigail's eyes opened wide as panic spread through her. "You will not tell him, will you? Please, I—"

"I won't say a word," Lady Chadwick promised solemnly, "if that is what you wish." Again, she chuckled. "Perhaps it would do him some good to have to chase after a woman instead of having them always swoon at his feet."

Abigail frowned. "Why would he chase me if he dislikes me?"

Lady Chadwick wiggled her eyebrows, amusement colouring her cheeks. "Oh, that I cannot say for I gave my word. However, be assured that he will seek you out. All I ask is that you give him a chance. Nothing more. Will you do that?"

Completely overwhelmed, Abigail nodded, her gaze suddenly drawn to the tall dark-haired man entering the ballroom.

As though the two of them were magnets, as though he knew exactly where she was, his gaze found hers and Abigail's breath caught in her throat.

Never had she truly looked at the many gentlemen vying for her hand. Never once had she asked herself whether she could like them. Always had her mind been made up by their interest in her dowry alone.

Could Winif—Lady Chadwick...oh, blast it! Could Winifred be right? Would they suit each other? And even if, did she even want a husband here and now? Or was it too soon? Too soon to know who she was and what she wanted? After all, grief had a way of clouding one's heart and mind. What if she decided now, only to realise down the road that she had been wrong? What would she do then?

No, it would be safer to continue her masquerade as Winifred had called it. If her brother would truly seek her out, she would not make it easy for him.

Perhaps that was wise. If he truly cared, he would have to fight for her.

A soft smile came to Abigail's face.

No one had ever fought for her. Not the way her parents had fought for each other.

But did she want him to?

6

A BROTHER'S SUFFERING

ideous.

There was no other word for it. The woman looked hideous. As though a bucket of mud had been dumped over her. No, not a bucket. A cartload.

Although Griffin had to admit he knew very little about women's fashion, he could not fathom why anyone would voluntarily choose such a hideous gown. Or such a coiffure. It looked like a bird had made its nest on top of her head, feathers sticking out every which way.

Shaking off a sense of dread, Griffin turned his gaze away, his eyes beholding a more favourable young lady.

Dressed in a dark green gown that shimmered in the light from the chandeliers, her golden hair framing her soft face in smooth waves and dancing curls, Lady Adeline, daughter of the Earl of Kingston, danced past him in the arms of a gentleman. The moment her gaze caught his, she smiled, and Griffin only too well remembered the night of the New Year's ball at Stanhope Grove.

Then, he had been taken with her ethereal beauty, almost

forgetting his promise to his sister of scouting the ballroom for eligible bachelors. Instead, he had asked Lady Adeline to dance, and it had felt heavenly.

"Not her," his sister spoke from behind him, the touch of a warning in her voice.

Inhaling a slow breath, Griffin faced her. "Why not?"

Winifred's gaze narrowed as she turned scrutinising eyes to the young woman in the dark green dress. "I admit she's beautiful," she finally said, now turning those scrutinising eyes on her brother. "But that's as much as you know about her, isn't it?"

Griffin shrugged. "Perhaps. But that can easily be changed."

"How often have you danced with her?" Winifred questioned, her gaze calculating as she watched him. "I know you met her at the New Year's ball. However, I've seen you with her several times since then. Can you tell me who she is?"

Griffin frowned. "Lady Adeline. She's Lord Kingston's daugh—"

"I know," Winifred interrupted.

"Then why do you ask?"

"I didn't ask you for her name," his sister huffed as though he was the greatest idiot to ever walk the earth. "I wanted to know what kind of a person she is." When Griffin hesitated, she prompted, a self-satisfied twinkle in her eyes, "Well?"

Annoyed with his sister's overbearing attitude as though there was nothing she did not know, Griffin straightened. "There have not been that many opportunit—"

"So, you don't know? Nothing?"

Gritting his teeth, Griffin glared at his sister. "Have you always been this irritating? If so, I cannot recall. Perhaps being married does not become you."

Winifred laughed, slipping her hand through the crook of his arm, turning his attention away from the dance floor. "Oh, don't grumble, dear brother. All I'm trying to do is point you in the right direction."

"I doubt that very much," he growled, finding himself looking at Miss Abbott yet again. "Why?" was all he asked as he looked down at his sister. "Why her?"

"That is for you to find out," Winifred said mysteriously. "She's a lovely, young woman, and I assure you that the two of you have a lot in common."

"Seriously?" Griffin demanded, remembering the many mishaps that seemed to befall Miss Abbott.

"Seriously," his sister confirmed, the tone in her voice not allowing for an argument. "Now, go ask her to dance. And wipe that scowl off your face."

Reminding himself that he had promised Winifred to give Miss Abbott a chance, Griffin squared his shoulders and commanded his feet to carry him in the direction of the young woman with the hideous dress. They complied, however, reluctantly.

As he drew near, Miss Abbott's head swiveled around, and for a short moment, Griffin thought to see a hint of nerves fluttering over her face. However, within the blink of an eye, it was replaced by a look of haughty superiority he had seen on her face before. He could not fathom how she had ever come to possess such a high opinion of herself. Was she not aware of the mayhem she caused?

Relieved to see her hands empty—no glass that could be conveniently dumped down the front of his shirt—Griffin stopped in front of her, inclining his head and smiling at her with what he hoped was an amiable sort of grimace. "Good evening, Miss Abbott. May I have the next dance?"

For a second, she seemed to glance over his shoulder at someone or something and the left side of her mouth curled up into the barest suggestion of a smile he had ever seen. Then, though, it was as though a veil fell over her grey eyes because they lost their humorous gleam and became sharp…and yet unseeing in a way. "How kind of you to ask, my lord." Her gaze narrowed. "Allow me to ask. Have we met before?"

Griffin tensed, displeasure pulsing through his veins. "Indeed. I had the…pleasure of making your acquaintance a few days ago at my sister's home. Lady Chadwick."

"Oh, yes, I remember now." Nodding, she gestured wildly, her left hand flying by the tip of his nose, missing it not by much. "You were the man with the serious scowl. Griffin, isn't that right?"

Griffin's muscles tensed to the point of breaking. Not only did she dare to address him so informally, but she also had the nerve to suggest that he was easy to forget. Did she truly only remember the way he had frowned that day? Was that all she remembered? For some reason, it bothered him to be thought of so lowly. Did he generally make a bad first impression? If so, he had yet to notice.

50

Forcing the corners of his mouth to stay up, Griffin instead clenched his hands, hoping to relieve some of the tension. "That is correct, *Miss Abbott*," he stressed, hoping to remind her that they were not on such intimate terms as to address each other by their given names.

The young woman, however, seemed quite oblivious as she suddenly grabbed his arm and all but dragged him onto the dance floor. "I do love to dance," she chatted happily, her voice a bit too shrill to be considered pleasant. "And if I dare say so myself, I'm quite the proficient. Unfortunately, I often find myself surrounded by less skillful dancers, which often robs me of the joy it usually brings." As though to disprove her own point, she moved contrary to the rhythm of the music, her steps too slow, and a moment later, her foot came down on his hard.

Griffin suppressed a groan. If he did not know any better, he would have thought she had done so on purpose, her heel digging into his flesh, almost crushing his toes.

In consequence, the inconvenience of stepping on his foot threw her off balance, and she tumbled sideways. If he had not been a gentleman, Griffin would have let her fall. However, he dared not, instead he caught her swiftly, releasing her the moment she had both feet back under her.

"My goodness," she exclaimed, drawing in a sharp breath. "I believe you would benefit from some dance lessons, my lord. Have you ever learnt? I can only recommend it as it would improve your enjoyment—as well as your partners—considerably."

"I shall keep that in mind," Griffin forced out through gritted teeth, silently counting the seconds until the dance was over. What was his sister thinking? Had she lost her mind? Ought he to have her committed to an asylum?

Quickly taking his leave of Miss Abbott as soon as he dared, Griffin crossed the ballroom in large strides, his gaze locked on his sister's, his blood boiling hot as he saw the amused gleam in her eyes. "I'm glad you find my misery entertaining," he hissed into her ear as he came to stand beside her.

Winifred laughed. She laughed! "Oh, dear brother, you suffer more than you need to!"

"That's what I've been saying," he agreed, trying to force calming breaths down his throat. "Then let us agree that Miss Abbott is not the right woman for me and move on, shall we?"

Grinning, Winifred shook her head. "That is not at all what I meant to say."

"What then?" Griffin growled, glimpsing Trent heading their way, a glass of wine in each hand.

"You are intent on disliking her," Winifred accused, "and therefore, you are miserable because that is what you expect."

"I doubt there is anyone on this planet who would enjoy her company."

"I do," Winifred objected as Trent held out a glass to her, his gaze narrowed as he looked back and forth between them. "Miss Abbott, is it?" he asked, a slight chuckle in his voice as he spoke.

Griffin could have throttled him. "As I've already said to my sister: I'm glad my misery entertains you."

Trent laughed, shaking his head. "Oh no, as tempted as I am, I will not get in the middle of this."

Exhaling a deep breath, Griffin took a step back. "If you'll excuse me, I'll find some more pleasurable company." And with that, he turned on his heel and marched off. Perhaps Miss Adeline would fancy a dance!

7

PERSEVERANCE

ying awake, Abigail remembered the moment Lord Amberly had asked her to dance. Indeed, he had looked like all the others, determined to pursue her despite their own inclination not to. However, the look in his eyes had been…amusing. He had seemed on the brink of throttling her, and on some level, Abigail had to admit that she had enjoyed seeing such unrestrained emotion.

At least, it had been honest.

Even if his words had not been.

Still, the emphasis in his tone had not been lost on her. He had greatly disapproved of her calling him by his given name. As did her grandfather. Still, there was very little they could do to sway her. After all, it was quite an effective tool in angering those one wished to anger.

Three days later, Abigail found herself seated in the breakfast parlour, staring across the table at her aunt as she picked at her food, her kind eyes dull and distant. "Is something wrong?" Abigail asked, deep concern in her heart for the only family member who had come to care for her.

53

Blinking, Aunt Mara looked up. "I'm sorry, dear. I did not mean to be so taciturn."

"I'm not complaining, Aunt Mara," Abigail stated. "I'm worried. Tell me what has you looking so forlorn."

"It is nothing," her aunt replied, waving her hand in dismissal.

Crossing her arms in front of her chest, Abigail glared at her aunt. "Whenever people say it's nothing, it's always something."

Looking up, Aunt Mara held her gaze.

"Tell me."

"I was simply..." She licked her lips, her fingers playing with her teaspoon. "I was merely thinking of my son, my grandchildren."

"You miss them."

Aunt Mara nodded.

"Why don't you call on them?"

Her aunt's eyes widened, and she instantly shook her head. "I could not. My son is...rarely home these days, and...I would not wish to disturb his wife."

Abigail's gaze narrowed. "She does not want you to see your grandchildren, does she? She's still angry with you for the counsel you provided your son."

With wide eyes, Aunt Mara looked at her. "How do you know this?"

Abigail shrugged. "Grandfather told me." Chiding herself for not pursuing this further, Abigail leaned forward. "We should go see them."

Again, Aunt Mara shook her head. "I don't want to cause any trouble. I—"

The door opened, admitting the duke inside and cutting their conversation short.

With barely a nod to them, he took his seat at the head of the table. By now, Abigail knew that her grandfather liked to do things a certain way. Namely, his way. And upon enquiry, he had informed her that he took his meals whenever he chose. *No one tells me what to do or when to do it!*

As though to prove himself true to his word, he always appeared at different times.

"How was last night's ball?" he enquired, watchful eyes on Abigail as he reached for his teacup. "Have you received any more proposals?"

Looking at her grandfather, Abigail could have sworn that there had been a touch of humour—sarcasm even—in his voice, and she tried to recall if her grandfather had ever seen her dressed to her *dis*advantage when heading out into society. Since he rarely attended any events held throughout the season—*why would he object himself to such torture?*—Abigail was certain that he had not. Then how had he learnt of her strategy? Because judging from the slight twitch in his upper lip, he had!

Feigning nonchalance, Abigail shrugged. "It was an evening like any other, Grandfather." Smiling at him, she noticed with delight the slight narrowing of his eyes when she did not address him as *your grace.* "Quite uneventful."

"Then why do you attend?" the duke asked unexpectedly. "If you despise these events, simply stay home."

Taken aback, Abigail tried to determine her grandfather's reasons for uttering such a suggestion. Did he not want her to mingle? How else was she supposed to secure a husband? Was not that what he wanted? "I admit that these events are somewhat tiresome," she finally said, deciding that the truth would be a refreshing choice. "However, sitting at home every night with no one to speak to would also not be my idea of an enjoyable night. In general, I like being around people. However, whether or not I enjoy their company is a matter of quality."

With an unintelligible grumble, her grandfather nodded his head. Had they just agreed on something?

Abigail shook her head. Apparently, strange things did happen after all…at least on occasion.

"Did you not enjoy dancing with Lord Amberly?" Aunt Mara asked, her gaze as watchful as ever. "I must say you looked quite pleased when he asked you to dance."

"Lord Amberly?" her grandfather enquired, his sharp eyes once more shifting to her face. "I knew his father," he continued in a grumble, his gaze turning back to the teacup in his hand. "The men in his family possess reason and a sense of honour." He inhaled deeply as the strong aroma of the warm liquid wafted upward. "I would not refuse my consent if he were to ask for your hand."

Momentarily too stunned to reply, Abigail found herself staring at her grandfather, unable to avert her eyes. What had happened in the last few seconds? Only a moment ago, she had thought her grandfather had taken a step back from his marriage plans for her. However, now, he had taken a leap forward. That man continued to confuse her!

Swallowing the lump in her throat, Abigail reached for her own teacup, doing her best to sound unimpressed. "It was…diverting," she admitted, a bored tone in her voice. "However, I received the distinct impression that his attentions were already otherwise engaged." Only too well did Abigail remember the golden-haired beauty in the emerald gown Lord Amberly had swept onto the dance floor after fleeing her company. She had to admit her strategy had worked a little too well that night! With envious eyes, Abigail had watched the couple share a beautiful dance, their eyes glowing and their lips curved upward into amiable smiles. Would she ever experience anything like it? Or was she doomed to chase away any man who dared approach her?

For a short moment that night, Abigail had not been able to remember why she did so. Perhaps her heart was beginning to heal. After all, she could not continue her life mourning her father's passing, could she? No, that would not be right. He would never have wanted that for her. After all, he had recovered—at least as far as possible—after her mother's untimely death, had he not?

Suddenly taking note of two sets of eyes on her, Abigail set down her teacup and lifted her chin. "I doubt he will call on me, so there is truly no point in discussing him."

A slight chuckle escaped her grandfather's lips, and even Aunt Mara turned to him with a confused frown on her face. "Have you already made plans for this afternoon?"

A moment later, there came a knock on the door and Orwel strode into the room, bowing to her grandfather and then addressing her. "This was delivered for you earlier this morning, miss."

Abigail glanced from Orwel to her grandfather, noting that there was not a hint of surprise on the old man's face.

Earlier this morning?

How long ago had the letter arrived? Had her grandfather held it back to be delivered at the perfect moment? Looking at him through narrowed eyes, Abigail thought to detect a touch of amusement in his eyes. Did he have a strategy of his own? One that factored hers in? Was he trying to undo her attempts at driving away her suitors? So far at least, she had not noticed anything.

Taking a deep breath, Abigail unfolded the sheet of paper for that's what it was. A simple sheet of paper. On its own. Not in an envelope. But surely, it had arrived in one, had it not?

Dear Miss Abbott,

I would be honoured if you'd allow me to take you for a drive through Hyde Park later this afternoon. I shall come by to collect you at four.

Yours sincerely,

Lord Amberly

"As I said," her grandfather broke into her stunned silence, "I do believe him to be a fine young man, and, therefore, I heartily give my permission. Do have fun."

Out of her grandfather's mouth, these words seemed like a joke, and Abigail looked up, wondering if her ears had deceived her. Judging from the triumphant gleam in the old man's eyes, they had not.

"What if I do not wish to go?" Abigail demanded, annoyed with the way people tended to force their decisions on her. Was she not to have a say in the matter?

"I do believe it would do you good to get out of the house for a little while, my dear," her aunt interjected at the most inconvenient of times.

"I do get out of the house," Abigail objected, casting a warning glance at Aunt Mara, which the older woman chose to ignore.

"Nonsense," her grandfather decided. "You cannot refuse him." Then he rose from his chair—apparently tea was enough that morning—and left the room, effectively ending the discussion.

Sighing, Abigail stared at the small note in her hands. Naturally, it did not contain a compliment of any kind or a small declaration of his affections. After all, he did not care about her, about who she was. All he saw was her dowry and the connection to her grandfather's name and family.

Nothing more.

Abigail could not deny that she was somewhat disappointed by that realisation.

Because I thought you would suit each other. Had Winifred been truthful? But how could she know if Abigail herself could not see it? Still, she had to admit she knew nothing of Lord Amberly. As little as he knew about her. Perhaps she truly ought to keep an open mind.

Perhaps.

8

AN AFTERNOON AT HYDE PARK

ith a block of ice firmly settled in his stomach, Griffin arrived at Lord Ashold's imposing townhouse, questioning his sanity at going along with his sister's demands. Was he being a fool? Most likely. Still, he could not refuse her.

He was honour-bound.

Bloody hell.

As he stepped into the entrance hall, a shrill voice drifted down the winding staircase from the upper floor, and Griffin cringed, feeling the desperate need to turn around and flee the premises.

However, he did not. He could not go back on his word.

Bloody hell.

Footsteps approached, and he reluctantly lifted his head to spot Miss Abbott descending the stairs in large strides before the butler could even show him to the drawing room. Dressed in a pale aqua green gown, the sleeves and hem set off in a brilliant red, she rushed toward him as though the devil was behind her. "Oh, Lord Amberly, how good of you to come," she exclaimed in that high-pitched voice that seemed to drill small holes into his brain with every word she spoke. "It was so lovely of you to invite me out on such a brilliant day. You don't mind if my aunt comes along, do you?"

Taken aback by the speed with which the words flew out of her mouth, Griffin had no time to answer before she prattled on, not waiting for a reply. Glancing up the stairs, he took note of the dowager marchioness, dressed in mute colours. Unlike her niece, she moved with grace and elegance, two attributes entirely lost on the young woman pulling on an orange coat and donning a dark blue bonnet. Was this woman colour blind?

Still stunned, Griffin could hardly get a word out before Miss Abbott rushed out the front door, her face lifted to the sky and her eyes closed momentarily as she smiled at the sun. "It truly is a beautiful day for walk, do you not agree?"

A walk? Glancing at his chaise parked at the kerb, Griffin walked down the front stoop as though in a trance. No, he had not intended to walk through Hyde Park. Still, as the dowager marchioness was to accompany them, there was no other choice.

As though he was not there, Miss Abbott continued down the street, pulling her aunt along. Following them like a dog, Griffin cursed his sister. After all, she could not possible have been serious? In fact, by now, Griffin was entirely convinced that Miss Abbott was widely referred to as the most awful woman in England with very good reason.

She was in a word -- awful.

As they proceeded toward Hyde Park, Griffin noticed how the dowager began to drift sideways, increasing the space between her and her niece. In addition, her steps grew smaller so if her niece did not wish to outrun her, she would have to pace herself. Step by step, she maneuvered Griffin to Miss Abbott's side and before he knew it, the young woman had her arm through the crook of his with her aunt trailing along behind them.

Although Griffin had no desire to get any closer to the young woman than necessary, he had to admit that he was truly impressed with the dowager's subtlety. After all, judging from the endless stream of words out of Miss Abbott's mouth, she did not even seem to have noticed.

"Oh, what a beautiful day!" she exclaimed for the tenth time that day, her right arm gesturing wildly at the scenery around them. "I cannot wait for spring. I simply adore flowers. All those colours, bright and brilliant. Oh, they so lift my spirits! I truly miss them in winter. I mean, I try my best to dress colourful, but there is only so much one can do. I must say I'm truly disappointed that not more young women dare to display such vibrant colours. It's such a shame."

Griffin swallowed, praying for the opposite. He could only hope that her tendency to mismatch colours would not turn into a trend. He doubted it very much, but one could never be certain.

"I love sunflowers. They're so cheerful," she continued as they proceeded down the path toward the Serpentine. "What about you, my lord? What is your favourite flower?"

At a loss, Griffin swallowed. Did he have a favourite flower? Not that he could recall.

Luckily, Miss Abbott was not in need of a reply to keep their *conversation* going. "But roses smell so wonderful and violets…" For the next minutes, she prattled on about every flower she had ever seen: their colours, their scents, the softness of their petals…

Griffin groaned inwardly, certain he had found his way down into hell. If this was not torture, he did not know what was!

Blowing out a breath, Miss Abbott shook herself, her nose scrunched up. "It's quite chilly after all," she said as they came to stand beside the glistening waters of the Serpentine. "Perhaps it was a bit premature of you to suggest a stroll through the park after all, my lord."

Griffin frowned. Had *he* truly suggested a stroll? He could not recall that he had. Still, he did not argue, but grasped the opportunity she was offering him with both hands. "Then allow me to see you back home," he said, turning on his heel and back up the way they had come.

Unfortunately, Miss Abbott took that moment to stomp on his foot with such vehemence that he could not believe it had been an accident. Suppressing a groan, Griffin gritted his teeth lest the less than flattering words he had been wanting to say to Miss Abbott all afternoon flew out of his mouth.

"You truly ought to look where you step, my lord," Miss Abbott chided him. "You almost tripped me. My beautiful dress could have been ruined."

Pressing his lips even tighter together, Griffin had never been so close to losing his temper. One by one, he forced a deep breath into his lungs, doing his best to close his ears to the young woman's incessant chattering. Instead, he turned halfway back to the lake and let his eyes travel over two young children playing on its banks. The boy tossed pebbles into the water while the girl was picking daisies growing near the bank, handing a small bouquet to her governess.

"Aunt Mara, are you all right?"

Blinking, Griffin turned back to Miss Abbott as he felt her hand slip from his arm.

With a slight crease in her forehead, she started toward her aunt, who stood in the middle of the path, her pale eyes fixed on the children playing near the water. "Aunt Mara?" Miss Abbott called, her voice suddenly softer, gentler as she tried to get her aunt's attention.

The dowager inhaled a sudden sharp breath, blinked a couple of times and then turned to look at her niece. "I'm sorry, my dear. I simply…" Her voice trailed off as her gaze travelled back to the children still playing by the water.

Miss Abbott turned her head, her gaze following her aunt's. Then a soft smile came to her lips as she looked back at the older woman. "It's them, isn't it?"

Swallowing, the dowager nodded, her eyes filling with tears which she quickly tried to blink away.

Stunned, Griffin watched as Miss Abbott gently took her aunt's hand and tried to draw her forward. "Let's meet them."

The dowager's eyes widened, and she dug her heels into the ground. "Oh, no, I cannot. She wouldn't like—"

"You're their grandmother," Miss Abbott stated sharply, a hint of annoyance in her voice. "You have a right to see them." And with that, she marched toward the two children, pulling the dowager after her.

Realising that she had all but forgotten about him, Griffin watched with great interest as the two women approached the lake. As soon as the children's eyes fell on the dowager, they raced toward her, hugging her tightly, bringing fresh tears to their grandmother's eyes.

With a look of concern, the governess stepped forward, determined to interfere. However, she was no match for Miss Abbott. With a stern look in her eyes, she glared the woman into submission, words flying out of her mouth without a moment's pause.

Griffin could not help but smile as he stared at her almost transfixed.

Gone was the shrill, loud woman with nothing to say but nonsense. Gone was the self-involved expression in her eyes as well as the odd grimace that could hardly be called a smile. Gone was the clumsy woman who had stomped on his toes more than once.

In her stead, Griffin saw a young lady, her eyes aglow as she now gazed at the scene before her, the soft smile on her face speaking of honest delight at seeing her aunt so happy. She moved slowly, gracefully as she retreated, giving them a moment alone. Her cheeks shone in a rosy red, and her teeth toyed with her lower lip as she forgot the world around her, her only focus the woman she clearly adored.

Drawing in a slow breath, Griffin took a careful step forward, coming to stand next to her. With watchful eyes on her, he said, "They seem very happy to see each other."

Miss Abbott sighed, her gaze still transfixed. "They do, don't they?" she whispered as though to herself, as though unaware who she was speaking to. "Oh, look how happy she is. She's missed them. I could tell. But she never speaks about them. She's so afraid to—" Turning to look at him, Miss Abbott froze, and he could see in the way her eyes widened that she had just realised what she had done.

The moment she had seen the shock on her aunt's face, Miss Abbot's act had slipped from her grasp.

And an act it was, to be sure.

There could be no doubt about it at this point. The only question was: why?

Grinning at her, Griffin watched with delight as her cheeks turned an even darker shade of red. "You seem quite changed, Miss Abbott."

For a moment her lips pressed together, and she closed her eyes. Then he saw the corners of her mouth twitch before her lips spread into a smile and her grey eyes found his once more. "I suppose you're right, my lord," she said, a teasing tone in her voice that Griffin found quite intriguing. "Is there any chance we could forget this ever happened?" she asked bluntly, a graceful sweep of her arm encompassing the scene at the lake.

Laughing, Griffin shook his head. "None at all."

Miss Abbott drew in a deep breath, a hint of disappointment in her calculating eyes. Still, Griffin could not help but think that she was pleased with the opportunity to be herself. Her true self.

Knowing she would never tell him if he were to ask why she felt the need to put on this act, Griffin chose a different approach. "Are you aware that people refer to you as the most awful woman in all of England?"

He felt blunt to ask such a question. However, his instinct told him she would not be offended.

62

The smile that came to her face told him that he was right. "I am," she confirmed, a touch of pride in her voice as though it had been a great accomplishment on her part to be rewarded such a title. "Why do you ask?"

Griffin shrugged. "I was simply curious."

"And would you agree?" she asked rather unexpectedly, a new-found vulnerability in her eyes as though his opinion mattered to her.

Holding her gaze, Griffin drew in a slow breath. "I did agree," he admitted, "up until five minutes ago." A soft smile came to her lips, and she glanced at the ground for a split second as though bashful. "Now, I'm not so sure."

Delighted with the deep smile that came to her face, Griffin shook his head. How could he not have seen this? Did his sister know? Was that why she had insisted he give Miss Abbott a chance? For clearly there was more to this woman than met the eye.

A lot more.

And suddenly, he was determined to learn who she truly was.

9

AN ACT OBSERVED

ressed in a bright red gown decorated with large black buttons—turning her effectively into a ladybird—Abigail sat in her grandfather's carriage, watching her aunt twist and turn a handkerchief in the seat across from her. "You'll rip it in two," she warned, her voice teasing, hoping to distract Aunt Mara from the one thought that had occupied her mind since their afternoon stroll through Hyde Park.

Blinking, her aunt met her gaze. "I'm sorry, dear. I've been awfully distracted lately. I—"

"I'm not complaining," Abigail reminded her. "I'm worried. I want you to talk to me. Tell me what is on your mind, and I promise we shall do what we can to put you at ease." Inhaling a deep breath, she watched her aunt for another minute. "It is your grandchildren, isn't it?"

Swallowing, Aunt Mara nodded.

"Are you afraid it will be a long time before you see them again?"

Tears appeared in the older woman's eyes, but she quickly

blinked them away. "I know it will. She does not want me to see them."

"Your son's wife?"

Again, Aunt Mara merely nodded.

"Why do you let her?"

Wide eyes met hers.

Abigail sighed, knowing by now that it was not in her aunt's nature to seek confrontation to achieve her goals. No, she cherished peace above anything else. Still, the situation within their family could hardly be called peaceful. At best, it was a truce everyone had agreed upon, but none was quite happy.

As they walked into Lord Blamson's ballroom, Abigail vowed that she would speak to her grandfather as soon as possible and once more urge him to seek out his grandson. There had to be a way that Aunt Mara could see her grandchildren more regularly than occasionally happening upon them in the park. That was ludicrous.

After spending considerable time standing by the dance floor, exchanging the occasional observation with her aunt, Abigail found a young man striding toward her. Although she could see his displeasure at her appearance in the way his gaze slid over her, he still asked her to dance…only to regret his decision minutes later.

In turn, watching one of their own limp off the dance floor dissuaded the young gentlemen present there that night from venturing anywhere near her. Although relieved, Abigail could not deny that she was bored. What was the point of attending these events if one could not dance? Or at least socialise?

However, she was the most awful woman in all of England, was she not?

To move her feet, Abigail began to venture from room to room, her thoughts drawn back to Lord Amberly as he had grinned at her, utter delight in his eyes, asking her if she knew about the less than flattering name the ton had bestowed on her.

For a moment that afternoon, Abigail had enjoyed herself.

Allowing her gaze to sweep over the dancing couples, Abigail felt her lips press into a tight line as annoyance rose to the forefront. Why was it not possible for her to dance without appearing as though she was looking for a husband? Why did everyone assume a young woman's life revolved around finding a suitable match? Was there nothing more to life than marriage?

Oh, to hell with them all if they even thought for a moment she would live by their rules!

Spotting a young gentleman by the side of the room, unoccupied at present, Abigail marched toward him, her mind made up.

A hint of the fierce determination that burnt in her chest must have shown on her face, for the young gentleman blanched visibly when he saw her coming, his gaze shifting left and right as though looking for someone who would come to his rescue.

However, fortune did not smile on him that night, and so he found himself put on the spot as the most awful woman in all of England asked him for the next dance. What was he to say?

Seeing him hesitate, Abigail grasped his arm and dragged him onto the dance floor before he had a chance to decline by offering up an excuse to not appear impolite.

Although Abigail enjoyed the chance to move her limbs, dancing with an unwilling partner was far from enjoyable, and so her gaze continued to venture around the room, hoping to spot something—anything!—to distract her from the sheer boredom that had become her life.

Her gaze fell on a well-groomed lady perhaps ten years her senior. The woman's eyes had narrowed into slits, and her lips looked more like the snarl of a charging cat. Then she did in fact charge forward, her feet carrying her toward…Aunt Mara.

Abigail froze as she saw her aunt's face turn white as a sheet, her hands twisting into the handkerchief with an almost desperate need to hold on to something.

Outrage rose within Abigail at seeing her gentle, sweet-tempered aunt thus attacked, and without further thought, she abandoned her dance partner in the middle of a cotillion and rushed across the room to her aunt's side.

In the very moment that the woman opened her mouth—no doubt to spew her venom—Abigail stepped into her path. "Lady Bradish, isn't it?" she said sweetly, her eyes sharp as they held the woman's angry stare, certain that she was none other than her aunt's daughter-in-law. "It's so nice to make your acquaintance. My aunt has told me so much about you." After glancing at Aunt Mara and seeing a touch of relief on the old woman's face, Abigail turned back to her opponent, noting the initial confusion turn to comprehension.

"Miss Abbott, is it?" the marchioness asked, a hint of distaste in her tone. "I had heard you were in town. You seem to be quite the talk of the season."

Holding on to her feigned smile, Abigail ignored the hidden insult. "Oh, that is so kind of you to say. Yes, I've made wonderful friends already. One nicer than the other. I hardly know where to spend my time, but I promise I shall call on you as soon as possible. My aunt often tells me how fond she is of your two beautiful children." She clasped her hands together as though surprised by a sudden idea. "We should take them out on a picnic. Aunt Mara, what do you think?"

Taken aback, her aunt did not reply.

"Yes, that's a marvellous thought," Abigail continued, cutting off the marchioness as she opened her mouth to object. "I will send word." Beaming at the marchioness, Abigail then drew her aunt's arm through hers. "It was truly wonderful to meet you." And with that she marched off, all but dragging her aunt behind her.

Stunned speechless, Griffin watched as Miss Abbott guided her aunt away from the sour-looking woman, who he presumed to be the children's mother they happened upon at the Serpentine.

As he had been unable to get Miss Abbott out of his head, Griffin had spent the past two hours since his arrival at the ball observing the young woman, trying to make sense of her strange behaviour.

Indeed, throughout the evening she had acted as she always had, dressed to her disadvantage, oblivious to society's code of conduct and all but blind to the reaction of others. Still, now that Griffin knew it was an act, he could not help but notice the small signs of her true self lurking under the finely crafted mask she had chosen to wear.

And then she had rushed off the dance floor in the middle of a cotillion, leaving behind a rather stunned looking gentleman, and hurried to her aunt's side.

In that moment, Griffin had seen the young woman, full of compassion and loyalty, he had met that day at Hyde Park.

And his heart had overflown with pride.

Following the two women to the refreshment table, he watched as Miss Abbott put a glass of lemonade in her aunt's hand, urging her to drink it. "You look pale, Aunt Mara. Perhaps you need some air."

"Don't worry yourself, Child," her aunt replied, carefully sipping her drink. "I was merely...surprised at your sudden appearance."

Miss Abbott smiled, then shook her head at her aunt's understatement. "You're right. Lady Bradish is not very fond of you, which is odd, because no one in their right mind could ever dislike you, Aunt Mara."

Miss Abbot's aunt smiled, and Griffin thought to see a touch of red rising to the older woman's cheeks. Realising that the dowager marchioness was probably quite used to being overlooked and taken for granted, Griffin could only imagine what her niece's words, her utter devotion and loyalty, meant to her.

"Still, you should not have spoken to her as you did," the dowager marchioness counselled in a rather apologetic voice. "She might—"

"I was polite, wasn't I?" Miss Abbott interrupted, daring eyes meeting her aunt's while the twitch that came to her lips spoke of suppress humour. "You cannot deny that I said nothing offending."

"Of course not, Dear," her aunt agreed, her fingers clenching and unclenching around the glass in her hands. "Still, you ought not to have suggested a picnic, knowing that it would upset her."

Miss Abbott snorted, "I do not care whether that woman is upset. All I want is to not see you so miserable any longer." Nodding her head with determination, she grasped her aunt's hand. "I shall speak to grandfather again. I'm certain he will find a way to fix this."

The dowager's eyes widened. "I'm afraid he will not be pleased if you bother him with this trifle. I've never known him to meddle in family affairs."

"Meddle?" Miss Abbott gawked before she shook her head in disbelief. "I have to say you all have a strange way to look at family. It's not called meddling if you protect the people you love." The dowager was about to open her mouth, but Miss Abbott cut her off. "He cares for you," she said, causing her aunt's eyes to widen even further. "He will do this."

The dowager swallowed. "No one has ever been able to make him do something he does not wish to do."

Sighing, Miss Abbott laughed, "Yes, I've noticed he likes to appear like a cold-hearted monster. It seems to amuse him greatly. But mark my words, it is only an act."

Watching Miss Abbott and her aunt head out to their carriage, Griffin found himself quite intrigued with the young woman he had loathed to meet before. Her compassionate and loyal side appealed to him greatly, and he could not deny that she was fascinating when she did not pretend to be the most awful woman in England.

Descending the front stoop down to the pavement, Griffin kept his gaze firmly attached to the duke's carriage until it turned at the next street and was lost from sight. "I could like her," Griffin whispered to the dark night, keeping his thoughts firmly away from the realisation that he already did.

10

PAST PAIN

"Grandfather, I need to speak with you!"

Looking up at his granddaughter, the duke rolled his eyes as he set down the paper he had been studying. "Did your father not teach you any manners at all?" he grumbled, gesturing at the door to his study she had pushed wide open without bothering to knock. "This is a ducal household, and we have certain rules here."

Abigail smiled, closing the door and approaching the desk. "Oh, don't pretend you don't like me barging in here, Grandfather." She lifted her eyebrows in challenge and delighted in detecting a telling quiver in her grandfather's upper lip. If she was not at all mistaken, she would think he liked her.

A lot.

Clearing her throat, she reminded herself why she had come. "It's about Aunt Mara." Again, her grandfather rolled his eyes. "We met her grandchildren the other day at the park, and last night at the ball, the marchioness stormed toward her with a dark scowl on her face."

Her grandfather's gaze narrowed, and she thought to detect a hint of concern in his grey eyes. "What did she say to her?"

Abigail blinked her lashes, smiling sweetly. "Nothing."

Her grandfather's frown deepened. "Nothing?"

"Well, I happened to notice—"

"Ah!" her grandfather exclaimed, understanding lighting up his face. "I should have guessed. Then what do you need my help for?"

Leaning her hands on the top of his desk, Abigail met his gaze, hoping that she was not wrong, hoping that he could be swayed into helping his daughter-in-law. "Well, I—"

"Why don't you sit down? I cannot say I'm overly fond of having to crane my neck to look up at you."

Abigail snorted, "In the chair of torture?" Chuckling, she shook her head. "No, thank you. In this regard, your choices are fairly simple: either get a more comfortable chair or stand up."

Her grandfather's brows rose in surprise; yet, there was a touch of pride in the way he looked at her, a strange sense of recognition.

"But let's not lose focus," Abigail reminded herself as well as him. "About Aunt Mara. You need to speak to your grandson and fix this."

"How I am suppo—?"

"I'm sure you can think of something."

Holding her gaze, her grandfather leaned back in his chair. "This has been going on for years." He sighed, and a sudden sadness came to his eyes. "Sometimes it is too late to change things no matter how much you wish you could."

Straightening, Abigail swallowed. "Are you talking about my mother?"

Drawing in a slow breath, her grandfather nodded. "I made a mistake to let her go, to not go after her. I thought…" He shook his head. "I should have told her that…And then she died, and it was too late."

Feeling tears sting the back of her eyes, Abigail stepped around the desk, her eyes intent on the old man sinking into the large chair. His eyes held such sadness, such regret, as she had never seen them before. "She died so long ago, and you never sent word," she said, remembering a life wondering about the family she could have had. "Then why now? Why did you sent Aunt Mara to bring me to London?"

"After I learnt of your mother's death, I was…angry." He

shook his head as though to dispel the memory. "Then her loss sank in, and for a long time, I…"

Abigail nodded, feeling tears run down her face. "I know," she whispered, remembering the sudden blow of losing her father, of having him torn out of her life, of being left utterly alone.

Looking up at her tear-streaked face, her grandfather rose to his feet. "After your father's death, I received a letter through a Mr. Melton."

Abigail frowned. Mr. Melton? He had been an old friend of her father's. One he had not seen in years. How would he—?

"In it, your father…he begged me to look after you."

Abigail sucked in a sharp breath, her eyes going wide as her heart hammered in her chest. "He did?" she gasped, her hands shaking as she lifted them to brush the tears from her face.

Her grandfather nodded. Then his hand reached out for hers, slowly, tentatively, before it gently closed around her chilled fingers.

A sob tore from Abigail's throat, and before she knew it her grandfather swept her into his arms, holding her tightly as she cried painful tears for the father she had lost too soon.

"I should have written," he mumbled into her hair. "I'm sorry. At first, I could not and then…time passed, and at some point, I felt it was too late. I know I failed her as I failed you, but there is no changing the past. All I can do is give you all I have now."

Pulling back, Abigail looked into her grandfather's weathered face, his grey eyes full of regret. "But you haven't," she whispered. "You gave me a dowry, nothing more. But what I want…what I need is you…and Aunt Mara. We're a family, and we can help each other through this."

Blinking back tears of his own, her grandfather nodded. "You're right. You're right. I'm sorry."

"Don't be sorry. Help me."

Nodding his head, her grandfather squeezed her hands. "I will. Don't worry. I will take care of everything."

"Thank you," Abigail sighed, impulsively hugging her grandfather to her chest before stepping back, her eyes holding his with a new sense of closeness. "And if you don't mind," she added, a teasing chuckle back in her voice, "withdraw my dowry so I can dress like a normal woman again and not like an insect."

Her grandfather chuckled, "Oh, I don't know. I liked the ladybird. The bumblebee, too, looked quite spectacular."

Abigail's eyes widened. "How do you know what I wore? You never—"

"Don't allow yourself to be fooled by an old man," he chuckled. "I know everything that goes on in my house and beyond." He grinned at her. "How is Lord Amberly by the way?"

Abigail's eyes narrowed. "Are you still trying to find me a husband? Didn't I just say that—"

"I know," he interrupted her, his eyes urging her to listen, "and I'm not saying you need to choose a husband this season. However, I urge you not to discount all your suitors. There might be one among them who—"

"They want my dowry!" Abigail snapped. "Your dowry! They don't care who I am."

Her grandfather laughed indulgently, "Well, you're not making it easy for them to get to know you, or are you?"

Abigail rolled her eyes. "I had to find some way to discourage them. They were swarming around me like moths to a flame. It was unbearable. You cannot fault me for thinking of a solution."

"I'm not. I applaud you."

Abigail frowned. "Excuse me?"

"You're an intelligent, beautiful and—despite popular opinions—amiable young woman," he said, his eyes shining as he looked at her. "And I think it is not a bad idea to make them work for you. *You*, not your dowry," he stressed. "Still, at some point, you need to give them a chance to see you for who you are. How else will they ever have a chance to like you? The real you?"

"Well, it would seem they're not interested in that at all," Abigail huffed, getting slightly annoyed with her grandfather's overbearing attitude.

A knock sounded on the door, and upon her grandfather's call, Orwel entered. "Lord Amberly is in the drawing room awaiting Miss Abbott."

As her mouth dropped open, Abigail noticed a knowing grin spread over her grandfather's face that seemed to scream, *I told you so, didn't I?*

Swallowing, Abigail tried to find her voice. "I'll be right out," she told the butler, wondering what on earth Lord Amberly was doing calling on her again. Had that moment at the lake been enough to convince him that marrying her might not be as awful as she had had him believe before?

Well, there was only one way to find out.

11

A NEW PACT

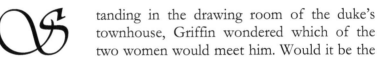

Standing in the drawing room of the duke's townhouse, Griffin wondered which of the two women would meet him. Would it be the hideously dressed, shrill woman who had squashed his toes on more than one occasion? Or rather the compassionate, fiercely loyal young lady whose smile he had seen in his dreams last night?

Quite honestly, Griffin preferred the latter.

Who wouldn't?

Still, there was no way to know, and so when he heard approaching footsteps, Griffin drew in a slow breath, every muscle in his body tense with anticipation.

Then the door opened, and in its frame appeared a young woman dressed in a simple, yet elegant gown, its subtle yellow fabric shining against the dark of her flowing hair, here and there pinned up, with loose tendrils dancing down to her shoulders.

Griffin breathed a sigh of relief…until his gaze fell on the dark scowl on her face. Swallowing, he greeted her. "Good day, Miss Abbott. It is truly a pleasure to see you again."

"The pleasure is all mine," Miss Abbott said as though in trance, her eyes narrowed as she watched him with no small amount of suspicion. "Please, do sit." Striding into the room, her long legs carrying her gracefully across the Persian rug, she kept her gaze fixed on his face as though hoping to unravel the mystery of his visit.

And surely it must be a mystery to her for as far as Griffin knew she had not received any gentleman callers in the past few weeks. Her act had driven them all away. Certainly, she had to be wondering what he was doing here, especially after her rather memorable performance at Hyde Park. Judging from the look on her face, she had thought herself successful in driving him away as well.

Then she cleared her throat, and a new determination flashed over her face. "May I ask what brings you here, my lord?" she asked, a sudden edge to her voice that had not been there before.

Griffin frowned, aware that she was displeased with his presence in her home. Had she decided to return to her act to rid herself of him?

An amused grin came to his face as he leaned back. "Do you care for an honest answer?"

His question seemed to surprise her for her eyes narrowed, and her voice returned to a normal pitch as though she had forgotten the role she had forced on herself. "Does your question imply that you generally do not speak honestly, my lord?"

Griffin laughed, "Do you?"

The muscles in her jaw tensed. "Well, I suppose honesty rests in the eye of the observer. I, for one, have observed that few people openly reveal their true opinions. Most hide behind civility, manners, social etiquette and, of course, their own ambitions." Her brows rose in challenge as though she dared him to contradict her.

Holding her gaze, Griffin leaned forward, resting his elbows on his knees. "Do you care to know what *I* have observed?"

For a moment, she hesitated, drawing in a slow breath. "Do tell."

"Well, I have to admit it took me a good while to make sense of you," he said, encouraged to forge ahead at her sharp intake of breath. "At first, your behaviour downright puzzled me. Why on earth would anyone act the way you did?" He shook his head, his lips twitching with amusement. "I wondered if there truly were people on this earth completely oblivious to how they are perceived by others. I could not fathom it to be true, and yet, you appeared to be one such unique individual." He chuckled, "But you're not, are you?"

Miss Abbott inhaled a deep breath, her hands curled into the fabric of her skirt. "What is your reasoning?"

"Everything changed that afternoon at the park," he continued, watching her face intently. "Your concern for your aunt overruled your *act*, and from one second to the next, you were a completely different person." He shook his head, laughing. "I admit I could not believe my eyes. For a moment, I thought I'd lost my mind."

Miss Abbott swallowed, her chest rising and falling with each breath as she held his gaze, waiting. "Do you plan on…sharing your opinion with−?"

"No!" he answered her question before it had even left her lips. His gaze held hers, and he could see a touch of anxiety in her grey eyes. Did she wonder about his intentions?

"Then why are you telling me this?" she asked abruptly, annoyance chasing away all concern she had felt before. "Why are you here? If your intention is to…secure my dowry, I might as well tell you now that my grandfather would never force my hand, and I would never accept a man who−"

"That is not why I'm here," Griffin hastened to reply as he saw the slight tremble in her hands. Did she truly think he would go over her head to enrich himself? "I do not want your dowry," he stressed, holding her gaze, willing her to believe him. "Nor do I *need* it."

Miss Abbott exhaled a slow breath, and some of the tension fell from her face. "So, you're not here to propose?"

Griffin shook his head. "Not at present," he said, surprising himself. Did he truly care for this woman? Or was it merely idle curiosity?

In answer, her eyes narrowed. "Then why *are* you here?"

"To get to know you," Griffin said. "I admit I'm fairly intrigued by your charade. It speaks of a strong will, tremendous creativity and no small ability to act. For the woman you portray to the world is nothing like you, is she? You invented her to protect yourself, to rid yourself of your suitors, men who wished to marry you to secure your dowry, is that not so?"

Swallowing, she stared at him, shock clearly written all over her face. And still, Griffin thought to see a touch of pleasure in her grey eyes as though a part of her revelled in the fact that he had seen behind her mask and noticed the real person underneath. "Is that all you've come for," she asked then, "to confirm you suspicion?"

Griffin chuckled, "Partly, I came because...I have no choice."

Her gaze widened, and he noticed a touch of curiosity. "Why is that?"

"A little while ago, I made a promise to my sister," he admitted freely, realising that he owed her honesty in return for stripping her of her mask, "and now she is holding me to it."

Miss Abbott swallowed. "What kind of promise?"

Watching Lord Amberly, Abigail noticed the amusement that never seemed to leave his eyes, and she felt herself relax when she failed to detect any kind of malintent. He wasn't laughing about her. Not at all. He seemed merely entertained by the situation they found themselves in. A man who would see the humour in the world. "So, are you bound to secrecy? Or can you reveal said promise?"

For a moment, he seemed to think her question over before his gaze intensified on hers. "Only if you promise not to reveal it to another? Let this stay between us, and no one else."

Intrigued, Abigail nodded. "From the way you speak, my lord, I must assume the worst."

"Oh, it is quite dreadful, I assure you." Still, there was a touch of mischief in his eyes that led her to believe he was teasing her.

"Well then?" she pressed, realising that she truly wanted to know.

Watching her intently, no doubt looking for her reaction, Lord Amberly took a deep breath. "Well, last fall, my sister suddenly decided that it was time she found herself a husband. However, she went about it in a most ridiculous way." He shook himself as though trying to dispel the dreadful memory. "She started to make lists of her attributes and intended to match them to those she could discover in London's eligible bachelors."

Abigail felt her eyes widening until she was outright staring at him.

Lord Amberly nodded vigorously. "That's exactly what I thought," he answered her silent reaction. "I thought it was a ludicrous plan, especially since she'd already lost her heart to an old friend of mine but refused to acknowledge it because—as she put it—they would not suit each other."

"You're referring to Lord Chadwick, are you not?" Abigail asked, feeling herself caught up in the story.

Lord Amberly nodded.

"So, you were able to dissuade her from her plan," she concluded, relieved for Winifred's sake. "They truly are a good match. I cannot imagine her with anyone else."

"Neither could I."

"Then how did you manage?" Abigail asked, somewhat surprised that he had a similarly calculating mind. "How did you sway her?"

Lord Amberly chuckled, "In order for me to have a say in her choice, I had to promise her a say in mine."

Again, Abigail's eyes widened until she stared at him, a deep smile on her face as she realised his predicament.

"Not my finest moment," he assured her. "Still, what was I to do? I could not in good conscience allow her to marry one of those mind-numbingly boring *gentlemen* because she could not admit to herself that she was in love."

Abigail felt her heart warm. "You love her very much."

"I do." A soft smile came to Lord Amberly's face. "She's my sister. As much as I want to throttle her sometimes, my happiness is irrevocably tied to hers."

Seeing the devotion in his dark brown eyes, Abigail sighed. Never had she known the love of a brother or sister. After losing her mother before ever having a chance to know her, her father had been her whole world. Until, he, too, had been taken from her.

"Are you all right?" Lord Amberly asked, the smile gone from his face, replaced by honest concern.

Abigail nodded, doing her utmost to blink back the tears that threatened.

"Do you...have any siblings?" he asked carefully, possibly suspecting a recent loss in her family. Had Winifred not told him?

Abigail shook her head. "My mother died in childbirth, and my father...a few weeks past."

At her revelation, Lord Amberly's eyes widened before utter sadness overtook his face. "That's why you came here? To stay with your grandfather?"

Abigail nodded, not knowing what to say. How had they gotten to this sorrowful topic? Would he leave now? Uncomfortable with a weeping female?

Closing her eyes for a moment, Abigail realised that she did not want him to go. Strangely enough, she found herself enjoying his company. Like his sister, he was one of only a few rare individuals who had managed to see *her*. Her true self. And as hard as she had worked to perfect her act, Abigail did not wish to live in the shadows any longer, hiding who she truly was.

"Our parents passed on about five years ago," Lord Amberly said into the silence. "Did my sister tell you that?"

Abigail nodded, relieved when he did not rise to leave. "She did. She said you left England after it happened, travelling the world."

Lord Amberly nodded. "We needed to get away. Everything around us only reminded us of our parents, of a past we had shared and a future that would forever be different." He sighed, "We needed a distraction, something to focus on." His gaze sought hers. "But we still had each other."

Abigail swallowed, "I have my aunt. She's wonderful."

"You care for her greatly."

Abigail nodded. "And my grandfather. He likes to make people think he is cold-hearted, but...he has suffered his share of losses as well. I suppose if there is no one else to live for, it hardens your heart."

Lord Amberly nodded. "Opening your heart to someone means the possibility of a new loss."

"Perhaps that was part of the reason why Winifred refused to acknowledge her feelings," Abigail suggested. "Perhaps she was simply afraid it would hurt more if she admitted how she felt."

Remembering the last time she had spoken to her friend—was she truly her friend?—Abigail could not help but address her doubts. "She said that...we would suit each other," she admitted, lifting her gaze to meet Lord Amberly's. "She said that was the reason she introduced us. Do you believe that is true?"

Lord Amberly grinned. "That we suit each other?"

"No, that that was her reason for introducing us."

Lord Amberly's gaze narrowed, a calculating look coming to his eyes. "You think she introduced us because she wanted to see me well settled? Because of your dowry? Your grandfather's name and title?"

Abigail drew in a deep breath. "She was the only one who tried to be my friend, and the moment I trusted her..."

"You felt betrayed."

Abigail nodded, her gaze shifting over Lord Amberly's face.

His eyes moved about the room, distant and unseeing, directed inward as though he was searching for the words to express what he wished her to know. Then they settled on hers, and Abigail felt her heart warm and her doubts disappear before he had even uttered a single word.

"Despite her rational mind and the strategic way in which she handles life," Lord Amberly began, shaking his head at the deep difference between him and his sister, "Winifred loves as fiercely as I do, and she is nothing if not honest. I do not for a second doubt that the reason she gave you was her true motivation for introducing us. Whether she is right in her opinion or not, I do not doubt that she believes it." He smiled at her. "I know she sees you as her friend, and as that, she would never betray you. I give you my word on that."

Holding his gaze, Abigail felt a new lightness spread through her body. After weeks of hiding and revealing nothing of herself, it felt utterly liberating to be honest with someone. "Thank you," she whispered, touched when his eyes lit up with relief. "This means a lot to me."

He nodded, a teasing grin on his face. "When you're not hiding behind a mask, your emotions are easy to read."

"Is that so?" Abigail dared him. "If you know so much, my lord, then tell me how I can rid myself of these mind-numbingly boring suitors—as you call them—without dressing up like a bug and squashing their feet every chance I get? Any brilliant thoughts?"

Lord Amberly laughed freely, "If I had any brilliant thoughts, don't you think I would have already found a way to circumvent my sister's meddling? I assure you she is as much a nuisance as your suitors are."

Enjoying herself as she had not in months, Abigail laughed. "Well, if we are indeed in the same boat, then I suppose we ought to work together to rid ourselves of your sister as well as my suitors. Perhaps together we can find a solution."

Lord Amberly nodded eagerly. "That's sounds like a marvellous plan. I—" His face froze in mid-sentence.

"Are you all right?" Abigail asked, frowning at the odd expression on his face.

Then his face split into a smile, and he slapped his hand on his knee in triumph. "I've got it!" he exclaimed, and his eyes settled on hers with a new sense of purpose. "What do you say we enter into a little pact of our own?" Abigail's gaze narrowed. "Now, don't look so suspicious! I assure you my intentions are most honourable…at least as far as our shared goal is concerned."

Suppressing a grin, Abigail said, "I'm not certain I dare ask what this pact encompasses."

"Then I shall tell you nonetheless." Grinning from ear to ear, he leaned forward conspiratorially. "You want to be rid of your suitors, and I want to placate my sister. Well, the solution is quite simple: why not act as though we're on the brink of getting betrothed?"

Abigail's mouth fell open, and yet, she felt her blood bubble with excitement as every fibre in her body urged her to agree. Being betrothed to Lord Amberly promised to be a lot of fun, even if it was only an act.

Frowning, Abigail wondered at her thoughts. She did not truly wish to be betrothed to him, did she?

"Are you all right?" Lord Amberly asked, interrupting her thoughts. "You have an odd look on your face."

Snorting, Abigail shook her head. "If you are to be my betrothed, you ought to work on your compliments. After all, no one will believe us if you speak to me in such a way."

"Granted," Lord Amberly conceded. "But only if you promise to be yourself. After all, if London's gentlemen believe you to be all but betrothed to me, there is no need to walk around looking like a bug, now is there?"

Abigail laughed, "I suppose not. Are you afraid it would ruin your reputation if you were seen with the most awful woman in England?"

"Terrified would be a better word," he teased, then held out his hand to her. "Do we have a deal?"

Holding his gaze, Abigail could not believe what she was about to do. Still, her right hand shot forward and grasped his before she had any chance of stopping it. "We certainly do, my lord."

12

A FALSE TRUTH

"Y ou look different," Winifred observed as she looked him up and down before her gaze came to rest on his face and her nose scrunched up as though she was smelling something rotten. "There is something odd about you tonight. You seem strangely cheerful, which—truthfully—makes me worry. After all, you've been wearing quite the tortured expression for the past few weeks. What are you hiding?"

Forcing an unobtrusive smile on his face, Griffin looked at his sister. "I have no idea what on earth you're talking about?"

At his reply, her eyes narrowed, and her nose scrunched up even more. Still, Griffin continued to smile as though he did not have a care in the world, his eyes gliding around the ballroom, wondering when his betrothed—well, almost!—would make her appearance. Perhaps he ought not to have insisted she come as herself. After all, his sister was already suspicious of his odd behaviour as she called it. Would she figure them out if they suddenly got along well? When she saw Miss Abbott in a normal gown that—?

The moment Griffin's eyes fell on his betrothed as she slowly made her way through the crowd—gaping at her and whispering to one another—he knew that he was doomed.

In more ways than one.

Dressed in a stunning, pale violet dress that made her grey eyes shine silver in the candlelight, she walked beside her aunt, her hair gently swept up onto her head, revealing her graceful neck, simple, yet, elegant silver earrings dangling from her ears.

In short: she was breath-taking!

And everyone saw it, gawking at her open-mouthed.

Not quite unlike him.

Unable to control his own reaction, Griffin knew that his sister was most likely putting two and two together in that very moment. Still, he was unable to tear his gaze from the vision before him to confirm his suspicions.

Her eyes glowed, and he could tell with one look that she enjoyed being herself, letting go of the act she had forced upon herself to defend herself against London's bachelors. Although Griffin detected a slight tremble in the smile that rested on her beautiful face—for once not stretched into a grimace—her movement spoke of relief, and the moment her silver-grey eyes fell on his, that smile grew deeper.

Griffin found himself draw in a slow breath as a slight shiver ran through his body. Ever since that day at Hyde Park, he had been intrigued by her. However, he had to admit that over the course of only a few days his interest had grown beyond mere curiosity and fascination. There was so much warmth and kindness in her eyes, and yet, they could appear as hard as steel whenever her protective instincts took over, defending those she loved.

Loved as fiercely as he did his own.

Had Winifred known? If he could have torn his eyes away, he would have chanced a look at his sister. Still, deep down, there was no doubt. Somehow his sister had seen something that had eluded him. Had he been blind because his own happiness had been on the line? Had his sister been right? Was a certain amount of objectivity useful when judging oneself as well as a potential match?

"If you'll excuse me," Griffin mumbled, finally noticing a bit of a gawking expression on Winifred's face out of the corner of his eye. Still, he kept walking until his feet had crossed the large room and carried him to *her* side.

"Good evening, Miss Abbott," his gaze barely shifted to her

aunt, "Lady Bradish."

"Good evening, my lord," Miss Abbott greeted him, a teasing grin on her face as she glanced around the room. "It would seem we have everyone's attention."

Griffin nodded. "So, it would seem indeed." He held out his hand to her. "Now or never."

Chuckling, she glanced at her aunt before sliding her hand through the crook of his arm. "Never is not an option, my lord," she whispered as he drew her toward the dance floor. "After all, I've already revealed my ruse. If you abandon me now, I shall be very cross with you."

When they stood up for a country dance, he held her gaze and as the steps carried them toward one another whispered, "Should I be afraid?"

Laughter seemed to bubble up in her throat, but she forced an expression of feigned seriousness on her face. "My lord, it would indeed be wise to heed my words. After all, you already are aware of the pain my heel can inflict, are you not?"

"Is this a threat?" he chuckled.

Shrugging her shoulders, she let her gaze drift heavenward. "A lady doesn't utter threats." A honey-sweet smile came to her lips as her eyes returned to his. "A lady merely retaliates."

Laughing, Griffin almost lost his step, "I shall consider myself warned."

Aware that all eyes rested on them, they finished their dance before taking a turnabout the room. Griffin offered her a refreshment, and they continued to talk. Mostly in hushed whispers as they did not wish to be overheard, but also because it gave the impression of a more intimate relationship. After all, they had a charade to play.

And to play it believably.

Still, Griffin could not deny that he was enjoying himself. More so than he had in a long time, and for a moment, he wondered if he would truly mind being betrothed to Miss Abbott for real.

Throughout the evening, Abigail was here and there asked to dance by a gentleman other than her fake fiancé. Although she felt no inclination to accept them, she did nonetheless for it was part of their plan.

As she twirled around the room on Lord Carlway's arm, Abigail did her best to portray a soon-to-be betrothed woman. More so, a woman swept off her feet.

"Are you enjoying yourself?" Lord Carlway asked, a luminous smile on his face that she had never seen once before when their paths had crossed.

"Tremendously," Abigail gushed. "It certainly is a beautiful evening, and Lord Amberly was quite the proficient dancer. I've rarely danced with a man who knew how to lead as well as he."

The light in Lord Carlway's eyes dimmed. "You look stunning tonight," he tried to change the subject.

However, Abigail could not allow that to happen. "That is very kind of you, my lord. In fact, Lord Amberly was the one to suggest I purchase a gown of this colour. He said violet would look lovely on me. Do you agree?"

"I certainly do," Lord Carlway bit out through clenched teeth.

Abigail smiled her best and utterly fake smile. "I shall speak to him of your kind words. He is such an attentive gentleman, and his return to London has greatly improved society's charm, would you not agree?"

Lord Carlway mumbled something unintelligible under his breath and when their dance ended took his leave with a few polite words. It would seem he had gotten the message.

"The man looked quite miserable," Lord Amberly observed as she returned to his side. "What on earth did you say to him?"

Abigail shrugged. "I sang your praises, of course. Only if they believe me to be quite thoroughly swept off my feet will they leave me alone, don't you agree?"

For a moment his gaze lingered on hers, and he inhaled an agonisingly slow breath before nodding his head in agreement. "I cannot fault your reasoning," he all but whispered, and Abigail could not help the slight shiver that ran down her spine. It would seem their charade was not leaving her unaffected.

"If you'll excuse me, my lord," Abigail said, unable to bear the weight of his stare a moment longer, "I shall see if my aunt needs anything."

He nodded, his gaze holding hers until she turned away.

Inhaling a deep breath, Abigail rushed away, feeling her cheeks warm with the intensity of the moment they'd shared. A mere few days ago, he had been a stranger, and now, it appears he knew her like no other. How had this happened?

Exchanging a few quick words with her aunt, who unfortunately urged her back to Lord Amberly's side, Abigail breathed a small sigh of relief when Lord Tennington stepped into her way, asking for the next dance.

As he led her onto the dance floor, Abigail noticed her fake fiancé approach from the other side, a golden-haired beauty on his arm. To Abigail's great dismay, her insides tightened and a sudden urge to claim him as hers rushed through her being.

Shaking her head, she swallowed. Where had these thoughts come from? After all, this was only a charade.

Trying to focus her mind, Abigail smiled at Lord Tennington. Still, her thoughts continued to drift back to the man down the line, smiling at the golden-haired beauty.

When Lord Tennington addressed her, Abigail reminded herself of her part of the plan and fell back into her role of the adoring betrothed. As before, her utter admiration of another man did the trick, and as soon as the dance ended, Lord Tennington rushed off the dance floor.

Breathing a sigh of relief, Abigail let her gaze travel over the room, searching for her aunt. Perhaps it was time to head home. After all, her feet were beginning to hurt.

"May I have this dance?" an all too familiar voice asked from behind her, sending an equally familiar shiver down her back. Abigail drew in a steadying breath before she turned and met his dark brown eyes.

Lord Amberly's gaze held her in place as he offered her his hand.

Slipping her own into his, Abigail almost flinched as the first notes of a waltz began to play and Lord Amberly stepped toward her, his dark gaze still holding her immobile, and slid his hand onto her back.

Then they began to move to the music, and the rest of the world disappeared.

"I will never understand," Lord Amberly whispered, the words falling from his lips, "how these men can allow themselves to be discouraged so easily." A soft grin tugged at his mouth. "Still, I am not complaining."

Abigail smiled, enjoying the soft pressure of his hand on her back. "Well, I suppose they know when a war is lost. After all, the way I have spoken of you would suggest that…"

"That what?" he pressed, his gaze almost drilling into hers as though his very life depended on her answer.

Abigail swallowed, her mouth feeling suddenly dry. "That I am spoken for." She drew in a trembling breath. "Is that not what we wanted them to believe, my lord?"

Although smiling, Lord Amberly's brows drew down into a frown. "I remember that you called me by my given name once or twice." A question rested in his eyes as he held her gaze.

"Few people appreciate having a stranger call them by their given name."

"You're not a stranger," he whispered, and the hand on her back drew her closer against him.

Abigail smiled, knowing only too well of what he spoke. "Am I not?" she teased. "Does this mean you want me to call you…Griffin?"

"Only if you give me leave to call you Abigail," he answered her tease, his voice light before he paused, his eyes drifting upward as though a new thought had suddenly occurred to him. Then his dark gaze returned to hers. "Or how about Abby?"

Abigail frowned. Still, she could not deny that his desire to address her thus pleased her. "That feels fairly intimate."

He nodded. "It does, doesn't it?" For a moment, he held her gaze. "Do you object?"

Abigail smiled. "I probably should," she finally said.

"Is that a *no*?"

Abigail nodded. "It is."

"May I call on you tomorrow?"

Despite digging her teeth into her lower lip, Abigail could not keep at bay the deep smile that came to her face. "You may," she whispered, seeing the same delight she felt reflected back at her in his eyes.

It would seem their charade was losing more and more of its most essential component.

The portrayal of a false truth.

13

A FAVOUR TO ASK

he next morning, Abigail woke with a smile on her face. For although she knew very well that they had agreed to merely assist each other with their respective dilemmas, she could no longer pretend that she was immune to Lord Amb...Griffin's charms. There was something about him that spoke to her. Not only was he kind and attentive, respectful and honest, but he seemed to respond to her in a way as though he had known her for years.

Had Winifred been right? Were they truly suited to one another?

Later that afternoon, Abigail watched her heart most carefully as Griffin picked her up with his open chaise and they took a turn around Hyde Park. "Is there a particular reason you chose to come here today?" Abigail asked laughing as her eyes drifted down the path they had walked together not too long ago.

Beside her, Griffin grinned, a teasing gleam in his eyes. "To be honest, I thought it would present the perfect opportunity to discuss your *methods of torture.*"

Laughing, Abigail felt her eyes widen. "Excuse me? My what?"

"Your methods of torture," Griffin repeated, bringing the horses to a slow trot. "I must say your act was quite refined and judging from the utterly shocked looks on people's faces last night, no one saw your...transformation coming." A slight frown drew down his brows as he looked at her. "How did you invent this person you pretended to be? All these details?" He shook his head as though truly impressed by such an accomplishment.

Abigail shrugged, unable to deny that she enjoyed his admiration. Never would she have thought it possible that someone would see her act as an accomplishment. "It was actually quite simple. I merely did what was considered in bad taste," she said shrugging. "We all have our little faults and imperfections no matter how hard we strive to be...well, perfect. All I did was pool them all into one being." Satisfied, she grinned. "Me."

Griffin laughed. "I admit you did well. That afternoon at the lake," he said, drawing the horses to a halt as they approached the Serpentine, glistening in the late afternoon sun, "I couldn't believe my eyes when the real you suddenly came through. I must have stood there for a small eternity gaping at you like a fool." He laughed, shaking his head as though he could not believe how blind he had been. "Still, I am grateful that I was here to see it." His gaze held hers as he swallowed, a touch of fear in his eyes. "I might never have realised who you truly were if I hadn't been here that day, if I hadn't seen you...change."

Abigail drew in a deep breath, realising how close they had come to simply parting ways without even realising what they would have lost. "Well, I suppose at least your toes must regret coming here that afternoon," she laughed, trying to lighten the mood. After all, he *had* been here that day, and everything had turned out the way it should have.

Had it been fate? What had been the odds of *him* being here with her and not another?

Griffin laughed, "I admit my toes were terrified of seeing you that day." Then his face sobered, and his gaze locked on hers. "I used to dread your company, but not anymore."

Abigail smiled. "Truly?"

Griffin nodded. "Now, I look forward to it. More than I ever thought possible." His hand gently came to rest on hers. "Knowing the real you was worth the pain. Any pain. I would not trade it for the world."

At his words, Abigail felt her heart dance with joy for she had to admit that deep down she had not been pretending from the moment they had agreed to help each other out. Even then her heart had recognised him as someone she could love.

But did she?

Quick footsteps echoed to Griffin's ears from the other side of the door, and without waiting for it to open, he knew it to be his sister. More so, he knew she was on a mission.

As expected, the door to his study flew open a moment later, and Winifred marched in, yanking her bonnet off her head and flinging it aside. "I demand to know what's going on here," she snapped, her eyes narrowed as she fixed him with a scrutinising stare. "You all but sneaked away at the ball the other night, and then I hear from Lady Hamilton that you were seen out in Hyde Park in the company of Miss Abbott."

Looking up, Griffin smiled. "Yes, I was."

Her eyes bulged. "Is that all you have to say?"

"I thought you wanted me to give Miss Abbott a chance," Griffin said, ignoring his sister's riled emotions. "I thought you'd be pleased."

"I am!" she huffed, the look in her eyes quite clearly stating that she was on the brink of throttling him. "But—"

"You wanted to be kept in the loop?" Griffin asked as he rose from his chair and stepped around the desk. "You wanted me to keep you informed?"

"Certainly!" Winifred snapped, her eyes widening in a way intended to make him feel like a fool for thinking otherwise. "Tell me what is going on."

Griffin shrugged, enjoying the aggravated look on his sister's face. "Nothing. I'm merely doing what you asked of me."

An annoyed chuckle rose from Winifred's throat, and she shook her head in disbelief. "Don't try to play me for a fool, dear Brother. I've told you so the night at the ball, and I will tell you so again. There's something odd about you, and I demand to know what it is."

"It's nothing." Griffin said, then walked past her to stand in front of the bookshelf, letting his eyes drift over the spines as he did his best to suppress a grin.

"Nothing? Don't you dare lie to me!" Although a tad shrill, his sister's voice held a clear warning as she stomped after him. "Abigail looked quite changed that night and you…you looked like a besotted fool even before she walked in…" Her voice trailed off, and she sucked in a sharp breath as though suddenly realising something that had been right in front of her all along.

Then he felt her hand curl around his arm a bit painfully—quite obviously she was agitated!—and jerk him around, her eyes wide as they searched his face. "What happened between you two?" she asked. "Were you the reason for the sudden change in her appearance? Are you—?"

A knock on the door interrupted his sister's questioning.

Annoyed, Winifred tried to compose herself as Griffin's butler entered, announcing the arrival of Miss Abbott as well as her aunt.

As a result, Griffin received one of the most glowering looks he had ever seen on his sister's face before he hastened out the door, hearing her footsteps on the floor behind him in fast pursuit.

Ignoring his sister's whispered questions, Griffin pushed open the door to the drawing room and felt his heart almost jump from his chest when his eyes came to rest on…Abby.

Ever since that night at the ball, he had thought of her as Abby. *His* Abby. That oddly reminded him of the way his oldest friend had always referred to his sister as Fred. A name that was only his. A name no one else was permitted to utter.

And in that moment when he walked in the door and their eyes met, Griffin knew that he never wanted Abby to leave. She belonged here. With him. And he would rather concede that his sister had been right than ever allow Abby—his Abby!—to walk away.

"Shall we take a stroll around the garden?" he suggested in a voice much calmer than he would have thought possible.

When everyone nodded their agreement, he escorted Abby out the door, followed closely behind by his sister and her aunt, both of which whispering to one another in hushed voices.

After donning their jackets, Griffin led her down the small steps leading down from the terrace into the garden, quickening his step to put some distance between them and their watchful pursuers. "I'm afraid my sister has become rather suspicious," he whispered next to her ear. "I doubt she will leave before she knows all there is to know."

Abby chuckled, her hand tightening on his arm. "She's your

sister, and she has a way of seeing the truth, does she not?"

Griffin nodded, enjoying the weight of her hand. "She does. At least where others are concerned. Perhaps we should have made the change a bit more gradually. She already suspects that your transformation has something to do with me."

Abby shrugged. "Well, she would be right, wouldn't she?"

Her grey eyes held his, and Griffin noted with pleasure that there was not a hint of concern or disappointment in them. Did she not mind that his sister was on to them? That she would most likely expect them to become betrothed for real?

Continuing down the path, they turned the corner and vanished behind a tall hedge, cutting across the garden. When they were no longer visible to their pursuers, Abby's hand slipped from his arm.

Disheartened by their loss of contact, Griffin stopped and watched her walk on a few steps as though she had not even noticed that he was no longer beside her.

Then her feet stilled, and he saw her shoulders rise and fall as she drew in a deep breath before turning to face him. Her eyes held his, and yet, she swallowed as though a lump had lodged in her throat. "I have a favour to ask you," she finally said, her hands wrapped around one another for support.

Frowning, Griffin stepped toward her, his heart hammering in his chest. Did she intend to end their charade? Had she noticed that for him it had ended long ago? Did she not feel as he felt? "Anything," he promised, hoping she would not ask him to let her go.

A soft smile drew up the corners of her lips, and yet, there was a touch of nervousness in her eyes. "I have a theory to test, and the way I see it, you're the only one who can help me prove or disprove it."

Not having expected that, Griffin found himself staring down at her. "A theory? What theory?"

"I shall tell you once I know the results," she promised, a hint of a teasing grin lighting up her face. "Will you help me?"

Aware that there was something he was missing, Griffin nodded nonetheless. "All right. What do you need me to do?"

For a moment, her teeth sank into her lower lip as she tried to dissuade the self-conscious smile that took control of her lips. "I need you to kiss me."

14

A THEORY CONFIRMED

bigail felt herself tremble as shivers shot up and down her body. Still, she held Griffin's gaze, seeing his utter surprise at her request, which then quickly turned into something more.

Something deeper.

Desire lit up his eyes, and they drifted down to touch her lips. Taking a step closer, he sought her gaze. "I assure you I'm most happy to oblige you," he whispered, a teasing smile lighting up his face, slowly putting her rattled nerves at ease, "if you are certain." The look on his face sobered, and she could see how much he cared for her. How had she not seen this before?

"I am," Abigail answered him, nodding her head up and down like a fool.

He held her gaze for another moment, seemingly indecisive, before she suddenly found herself swept into his arms. His right arm came around her waist while his left hand slid into her hair at the base of her neck. Then his lips touched hers in a soft, rather chaste kiss.

Welcoming his warmth, the touch of his lips, the feel of his embrace, Abigail found herself a bit frustrated with his restraint. Her fingers trailed down the side of his face and found the hammering pulse at the base of his neck. Why was he holding back?

When Griffin lifted his head, his eyes fluttering open, Abigail slung her arms around his neck and pulled him back down to her. Although her theory had been more than confirmed, she was quite unwilling to cease her explorations. After all, one could never be too certain, could one?

At her reaction, Griffin's hold on her tightened and he finally kissed her with all the passion she had hoped for. The world around her began to blur, and she would have sunken to the ground into a puddle of trembling flesh if his strong arms had not held her closer to his body.

Still, after a small eternity, he did pull away, chuckling at her small noise of protest. "What is your verdict?" he asked, his gaze holding hers as his lungs held his breath.

Abigail smiled, feeling her body hum with the knowledge she had gained. Then she swallowed and cleared her throat, trying to focus her thoughts. "Well, the results quite confirm my suspicions," she said teasingly, enjoying the smile that lit up his face.

"What suspicions?"

"That I lost my heart to you," she said without hesitation, her grin widening when she saw his mouth fall open at her boldness. "I keep wondering how it happened and when. I woke up one morning, and it was simply gone."

Holding her in his arms, Griffin sighed. "Did you find mine in its stead? I'm afraid I seem to have lost mine as well. Quite unexpectedly, I assure you."

As the world around her began to sing, Abigail closed her eyes, her teeth once more sinking into her lower lip, unable to contain the happiness that flooded her being.

"Would you in turn help me answer a question?" Griffin asked, the look in his eyes one of calm apprehension. When she nodded, he drew in a deep breath. "You must promise to answer honestly."

Again, Abigail nodded.

Again, he drew in a deep breath. "Do you want to marry me?"

Judging from the look on his face, Abigail had in fact expected a proposal. Still, what she had not expected was for him to ask what she wanted. Not if she would marry him, but if she wanted to marry him. "Why do you ask?"

A nervous chuckle escaped him, "Isn't it obvious?"

Laughing, Abigail sighed, "Appearances can be deceiving as you well know."

"That is true," he admitted, his gaze not wavering from hers. "I ask because…I love you. Is that not what it means to lose one's heart to another? Is that not what you meant?"

Abigail nodded. "It is. And I love you, too."

"I knew it!" Winifred's voice cut through the peaceful moment before she came rushing around the hedge, her eyes sparkling with triumph as she looked from her brother to Abigail. Next to her, Aunt Mara appeared, looking a bit ill at ease.

"See?" Winifred exclaimed, stepping toward them. "I knew you'd like her. Why didn't you trust me? I would never have steered you wrong."

Laughing, Griffin shook his head at his sister. "Would you get lost? In case you haven't noticed, you've just ruined a most wonderful moment."

Winifred's face turned a darker shade of red, and her hand flew to her mouth. Still, there was little to no regret in her eyes as she cast one last look at her brother and marched off, Aunt Mara in tow.

"Now, where were we?" Griffin mumbled, turning back to her, a light-hearted smile on his face. "Ah, yes, you haven't answered my question yet. And please, don't be discouraged by my nosey sister. If you want, we can move, leave the country, go somewhere where she'll never find us."

Her heart filled with delight at the close family Abigail could see in their future, and she looked up at Griffin and knew with perfect clarity what she wanted. "Don't you dare," she teased. "She belongs with us."

"Us?"

Abigail nodded. "Yes, us," she confirmed, feeling her heart beat faster at the utter joy that shone through his eyes. "As do Aunt Mara and my grandfather. They might drive us crazy at times, but they're a part of us. They're family, and we would never be the same without them. They shape who we are, and we do the same for them." A sigh escaped her lips as she sank a little deeper into Griffin's arms. "Grandfather told me this morning that he spoke to his grandson, Aunt Mara's son. He agreed to speak to his wife and ensure that his mother could see her grandchildren on a regular basis. You should have seen her." Closing her eyes for a moment, Abigail smiled. "I've never seen her so happy."

Tightening his hold on her, Griffin sighed. "Let's agree to always be honest with each other and fight openly...and not secretly behind each other's back. Secrets destroy trust, and once that is lost, there is no going back. Not completely. There'll always be doubts."

Abigail nodded, touched by the depth of his thoughts.

"How would you feel about a June wedding?" Griffin asked suddenly, the seriousness in his eyes replaced by a youthful eagerness that suited him well.

"That's in two months!" Abigail exclaimed, knowing without a doubt that she had no objections. "Aunt Mara would be happy to help us plan. It would make her happy to be included."

"But first," Griffin began as his eyes narrowed, a touch of apprehension coming to his face, "I need to speak to your grandfather and ask for your hand in marriage."

Abigail laughed, "He will not be surprised by your visit," she assured him, remembering how her grandfather had winked at her earlier that day when she had left the house with her aunt to go call on Griffin. "If I'm not mistaken, he knew well ahead of us that we would end up together." A snort escaped her. "Kind of like Winifred. Perhaps not only we are suited to one another, but also our families."

Griffin chuckled, "Perhaps you're right. Perhaps we've always been meant for each other."

Whether or not it was fate or coincidence, Abigail did not care. All that mattered was that they had found each other. How often did people who would fit perfectly into each other's lives meet but not realise it? How often did fate go unanswered because people were too busy, too distracted or too stubborn to see what was right in front of them?

Abigail could not deny that she had been one of them, and so had her betrothed. Still, they had been able to wrench their eyes open just in time before they would have walked out of each other's lives without a look back.

Never in a position to regret what could have been.

Because they would have never known.

Abigail whispered a silent thank-you to her father, whose letter had sent her to London in the first place.

To London.

And to Griffin.

EPILOGUE

About Two Months Later

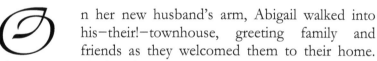

n her new husband's arm, Abigail walked into his—their!—townhouse, greeting family and friends as they welcomed them to their home. Smiling, she saw Winifred and her husband Trent, her friend's eyes aglow with delight to see her brother happily married. Aunt Mara seemed quite changed as well. Although she still stood back, far from the spotlight, her eyes no longer shone with sadness, but with joy, with hope, as she bent down to whisper something into her granddaughter's ear. And then there was Abigail's grandfather.

After their talk about past mistakes and the burden of time passing, there had been a silent understanding between them. Although he still appeared the cold, distant duke—and very much enjoyed the effect he had on others!—Abigail knew that he loved her. He had never said it. Not with words. His love for her was in the little things he did. The way he noticed her, saw her joy and all but pushed her toward it, afraid she would miss out and live a life of regret.

A life he knew only too well.

"Are you happy?" her husband asked, his voice low so only she would hear.

Abigail sighed, "I am."

For a moment, his gaze lingered on hers, taking in the small creases on her forehead, the downcast lids and bent of her head. "You wish your father were here, do you not?"

Abigail smiled. "As do you."

Griffin nodded, the same touch of sadness and regret in his gaze that Abigail felt in her own heart. "I do," he confirmed, "and I'll never not regret that they are not. Still, I cannot help but wonder if we would even have met, had they not been taken from us."

Taking her seat at the large breakfast table, surrounded by the people she loved the most, Abigail knew that he was right. Would she ever have come to London if her father had not died?

Abigail was certain that the answer was, *no*. She would never have gotten to know her grandfather and her aunt. She would never have met Griffin. She would never have fallen for him.

Good and bad did walk hand in hand, it would seem. No one could help that. Tears and smiles could never be without the other for how would we know the meaning of a smile if we had never learnt that of a tear?

Smiling at her husband, Abigail knew that she did not regret her past for it had led her here. Still, she could regret her father's passing without guilt over the happiness she had found in life. After all, he would have wanted this for her.

Not all regrets were dangerous.

Only those that were self-inflicted.

Others were merely memories.

Memories Abigail would cherish for the rest of her life.

ABOUT BREE

USA Today bestselling author, Bree Wolf has always been a language enthusiast (though not a grammarian!) and is rarely found without a book in her hand or her fingers glued to a keyboard. Trying to find her way, she has taught English as a second language, traveled abroad and worked at a translation agency as well as a law firm in Ireland. She also spent loooong years obtaining a BA in English and Education and an MA in Specialized Translation while wishing she could simply be a writer. Although there is nothing simple about being a writer, her dreams have finally come true.

"A big thanks to my fairy godmother!"

Currently, Bree has found her new home in the historical romance genre, writing Regency novels and novellas. Enjoying the mix of fact and fiction, she occasionally feels like a puppet master (or mistress? Although that sounds weird!), forcing her characters into ever-new situations that will put their strength, their beliefs, their love to the test, hoping that in the end they will triumph and get the happily-ever-after we are all looking for.

If you're an avid reader, sign up for Bree's newsletter at www.breewolf.com as she has the tendency to simply give books away. Find out about freebies, giveaways as well as occasional advance reader copies and read before the book is even on the shelves!

Thank you very much for reading!

Bree

A FORBIDDEN LOVE
NOVELLA SERIES

For more information, visit

www.breewolf.com

LOVE'S SECOND CHANCE SERIES

For more information, visit

www.breewolf.com

49607579R00064

Made in the USA
Columbia, SC
24 January 2019